Of the
Weird West

To Tommy!
The prettiest man I know
Rich Had

Edited by Axel Howerton

and R. Overwater

Coffin Hop Press

"The Gifts of a Folding Girl" © 2015 Scott S. Phillips
"The First Rodeo" © 2015 The Cenotaph Corporation
"Rosie's Chicken & Waffles" © 2012 Axel Howerton
"Bloodhound" © 2015 C. Courtney Joyner
"Dinner In Carcosa" © 2015 Sean Marchetto
"Death Is Daily" © 2015 Craig Garrett
"Cold Eggs & Whiskey" © 2015 Rick Overwater
"The Horse Always Gets It First" ©2015 Axel Howerton
"You Are The Blood" © 2015 Axel Howerton

Cover Design: © 2015 by Coffin Hop Press
Cover Image: Shutterstock/Seita/Markus Gann
Lettering: Rick Overwater

Published Worldwide by

Coffin Hop Press
Calgary, Alberta
Canada
www.coffinhop.com

First Print Edition:
April 2015

ISBN-13: 978-0-9936055-0-5
ISBN: 0993605508

DEDICATION

This one's for Forry, Dutch, the Rays,
And for all the ol' outlaws and cowboys…
Whatever damned galaxy they may hail from.

CONTENTS

INTRODUCTION

Tall tales of the weird west, that's what we got us here...

Whether it's were-wolves, choo-pee-cab-raws, stories from a different time and place—even dang ol' zombies—ain't nothin' like a fine tale and a good glass of whiskey to warm you on a cold night out under the stars. Funny things, them stars... They just keep on shinin' down, watchin'... waitin'... And once in a while, somethin' comes down out of that cold black void and lights up the midnight skies like nothin'' you ever seen. Then—especially then, friend—you want to be ears-up, wary like a jackrabbit.

Yessir, you never know when a book like this might come in handy. Some night, out under them funny stars, when the night winds call your name and that lonely coyote howls out to lord knows what up there on that big ol' moon... Somethin' like this might just give you the right idea to save yourself a little trouble of your own.

Knowledge is power, some wise sumbitch once said, and this kind of knowledge ain't easy to come by. The stories in this here book are all one-of-a-damn-kind. Special-like. Full of terror and wonder and all kinds of strange goings-on. Things you only hear about by campfire light, or in the darkest corner of the shadiest whorehouse saloon.

We certainly hope you enjoy 'em. If'n you do, go tell a friend or, better yet, buy 'em their own damn copy so they don't sneak off with yours.

So settle your behind, light up your brains, and 'git to readin'.

--El Cuchillo
Writer of the Weird Frontier
Spring 2015

Coffin Hop Press

THE FIRST RODEO

JACKSON LOWRY

"Were you born in a barn? Close the damn door."

"You're a cheapskate, Crow. You are the proprietor of this place? Throw another log on the fire. Or are you too lazy to even cut wood?" The cowboy leaned against the restaurant door finding it difficult to secure against the fierce Wyoming wind. "Ain't even winter yet and you already have this place so cold, icicles form on your nose."

To prove his point, the cowboy ran his sleeve over his nose to get rid of the drip forming there. With supreme indifference to hygiene, he snapped his arm out to get rid of the snot. The green knot, along with half frozen rain, slid off his slicker and onto the floor.

Crow looked the cowboy over, scowled darkly and pointed to a table closer to the fireplace. He had owned this restaurant for close to ten years and never got used to the bad manners some of the wranglers showed. Living out on the barren plains took the edge of civilization off a man, but there was no call to act like a barbarian in town. Not that Havelock was much of a town with only a hundred residents. It still rankled Crow when a patron showed no manners.

"What can I get you?"

The cowboy looked over the proprietor, nodding as he took in the details.

"I'm in off the Mr. Jansen's Triple D out north of town."

"I know the place," Crow said. "You have the sound of a Southerner. Texas?"

"I am a proud Texican," the cowboy said. "Me and two my two partners. They're not far behind me."

"You know my name, but then it's painted on the window right above the restaurant sign. What do I call you?" Crow knew what he wanted to call the son of bitch as he hoisted his boots up to the chair beside him. The spurs dug into the wood, making the next person to sit in that chair prone to splinters in his ass.

"Flaco's what they call me. The ramrod said you serve the best damn steak in all of Wyoming. Now, I'm used to the finest beef, being from Texas. The cattle that tromp northward along the Goodnight Trail 'bout have meat falling off their bones, their beef's so tender."

"You can eat somewhere else."

"The ramrod said you were the best because you were the only restaurant in town."

"It's real heartening to know that Jesse Llewellyn is smart enough to figure that out on his own."

The cowboy laughed. He leaned back in the chair, then shrugged out of his slicker as the heat warmed him enough. "I think the same thing about him. He's good enough with the herd, but he's not what you call a deep thinker. No imagination."

The door let in a new wintery blast. Two more cowboys came in, having the same trouble closing the door that their partner had. Crow had never seen them, either. The Triple D had hired a raft of new hands when the gold strike down in Leadville, Colorado, emptied half of Wyoming of men looking to hit it rich. Jansen had to make do with any drifter coming through.

But the Triple D paid decent wages, so Crow welcomed

its cowboys into his restaurant. Even if they were all uncouth.

"Come on in, boys," the seated cowboy said. "Got chairs waiting for you over here by the fire." He made a big deal of lifting his feet and dropping his spurs smack in the middle of the chain across from him.

Flaco let out a yelp when Crow reached down, took the edges of his chair and lifted. The cowboy was heavyset, belying his nickname, but Crow swung him and the chair around as if he didn't weigh an ounce. He deposited the chair to one side, leaving the other two chairs at the table open for the newcomers.

"What can I get for you gents?"

"Saloon's closed. That's why we come in here," the taller, thinner cowboy said, carefully choosing the chair his partner hadn't carved up with his spurs. His friend didn't show any such fussiness. "You got any whiskey?"

"Half a bottle of rye," Crow said. "My own stash."

"That's what I expected you to say. You can charge more for it that way." The first cowboy looked smug.

"Then I don't have a drop."

"Thanks for nothing, Flaco." The cracker-ass cowboy hit his friend in the shoulder hard enough almost to knock him from his chair. Crow vowed to not let appearances deceive him. The cowboy could turn sideways and disappear, but what was there had to be pure whipcord muscle. "I don't know about you and Slaughter but my gullet's so dry after a month singing to cattle, I could drink alkali water."

Crow fixed them up with a round. Each of the three downed the rotgut, then he poured another. To their credit the trio sipped at this shot, taking it easy.

"I reckon you three want steaks?"

"Grilled," agreed Flaco. "But I want mine to moo when I stick a fork in it."

The others agreed.

"Rare it is. I'll even give you my best. Throwed, hogtied and branded this one myself."

"You don't look like a cowboy, Crow."

"Why not?" Crow knew the reason and it rankled. He stood an inch under five feet but tipped the scales at close to two hundred. Most men thought it was fat under his clothes, but not an ounce of it was.

"Oh, nothing. Get those slabs of beef broiling, and they'd better not come from Pecos, Texas, either."

"Why not Pecos?" Crow frowned. The heavy bony ridge over his eyes tensed in a frown, making his eyebrows ripple like a pair of goosed woolly caterpillars. "My meat's better, but what's wrong with Pecos beef?"

"That's where the first rodeo was held, that's why. The meat would be tough from all them cowpokes kicking at the sides as the bull tried to ride 'em." The skinny one looked pleased with himself.

"That wasn't the first rodeo. That was in Prescott."

"Payson," said Slaughter. He glared at his friends. "You got shit for brains, Kenyon, if you think either Prescott or Pecos had the first rodeo."

"I know what I'm talking about. The boys at Red Newell's saloon put up $40 in prize money at Pecos. That makes it official." Kenyon worked on his rye. His Adam's apple bobbed in his scrawny neck as he swallowed in triumph.

"First silver shield went at Prescott." Flaco wasn't going to let any argument lie. Neither of his partners did, either. Crow saw this was the trio's usual way of passing the time and wasn't likely to break out in gunplay, though only Slaughter and Flaco wore iron at left hips, slung cross-draw style.

As he worked to get the cooking stove fired up and the slabs of meat on the griddle, Crow listened to the argument grow until it rivaled the whine of the wind outside. He hefted the bottle and pulled up a chair to join the three. They stared at him a moment, then at the bottle.

Kenyon grinned.

"You settle it, Crow. What was the first rodeo?"

Crow poured another round, adding one for himself. He savored the bite as the whiskey rolled down his gullet and warmed his gut. After a moment, he shook his head.

"You're all wrong. The first rodeo was a long time back. A very long time. I know. I was there."

"I feel a tall tale coming on," said Slaughter. He worked at his shot. In spite of his words, a grin crept to his lips. He and the others were in the mood for a story.

Crow was willing to oblige. It had been a long day, and they were his first customers. With the storm blowing harder by the minute, they might be his last for a spell. If the snow piled up the cowboys would be stranded for the duration of the blizzard. He had seen it before. He had seen about everything before and was feeling like he had to share some of it with these wranglers.

Greenhorns, almost. They thought they had seen it all and done it all. The oldest was hardly out of his teens.

"So where was this rodeo you're claimin' to be the first?" Slaughter helped himself to a little more of the whiskey put on the table.

"Wasn't more than fifty miles from here. Up in the Grand Tetons, it was," Crow said. He thought on it a moment, then added, "It had to be a couple dozen years ago."

"What was you then? Two?"

Crow smiled.

"I'm older 'n I look."

"You look older 'n dirt," Kenyon said. This let them laugh and loosen up a mite to appreciate his tale better.

"It wasn't like the rodeos now. You didn't just show up and say you wanted to do some roping or bulldogging. I had to earn the right to participate in the real rodeo."

"How'd you do that?"

"By doing all the things you think wins a rodeo now. Showing roundup skills. I broke one of the damnedest, worst bucking horses I ever did see. Sunfishing son of a gun. Burned the top of my head on the sun he rocketed up so far. All four hooves off the ground at the same time until I thought I'd end up on the moon 'cuz he bucked all through the day and into the night, never letting up. But I rode him. Broke him, too."

"You talking about that broke-down nag out back? We

seen it a time or two when we come into town for supplies for Mr. Jansen."

"Grandson of that horse," Crow said before he realized he was giving too much away. He took another drink. They weren't too good figuring out that meant the grand sire was close to thirty years in the past. "I was awarded the stallion, and I could have gone home then with my prize."

"But you didn't." Kenyon hiccoughed, leaned back and thrust his legs out toward the fire. Somehow a bit of wind crept past the door and across Crow's neck. He moved in the direction of Kenyon's feet. The fire warmed his body, but the memories were stone cold, the way they always were.

"I should have. If I'd had the sense God gave a goose, I'd have lit out, but I was feeling my oats and wanted to take on the world. Well, busting that bronco was my way in. Three railbirds caught sight of the way I looked and realized I wasn't like the others who showed up. Truth was, I recognized them as being like me."

"Short and stubby?" Slaughter laughed. Crow didn't. The cowboy was right. Those three might have been his brothers. If he had dug long enough, he knew he would have found more than one relative in their respective family trees.

"We rode deeper into the mountains until I got so turned around I hardly knew which way was up, much less out. We finally reached the valley."

Crow pictured it perfectly in his mind.

"There was a tall fence, a palisade, stretching fifty yards to pen up the critters inside."

"For the rodeo?"

"For the rodeo," he agreed. "We left our horses outside and slipped through a hole in the fence hardly that wide." He showed them with his hands, as if bragging about a fish he'd caught. "It was a tight fit, but it was a necessary one." In spite of the warmth from the fire, he shivered.

"There was an entire herd of fire-snortin' bulls waitin' fer you?"

"That would have been easier. These critters were ten

hands tall."

"That's not so much." Kenyon reached out and indicated a height of about four feet. "Mighty small, I'd say."

"They weren't cattle, and they weren't horses. I don't know what they were. Lizard things with teeth six inches long. And fast. The damned things were quicker 'n any striking snake I ever saw."

"So you bulldogged one and won the rodeo?" Slaughter snorted. "That ain't much of a story."

"I had to break another critter. This one was more 'n eight feet tall and had horns like this." He held out his hands as far as his short, muscular arms could reach. "More. The horns were longer than the other critters were tall."

He sipped at his whiskey. The cowboys fell silent and exchanged glances. Kenyon started to leave, but the other two took deep sniffs of the cooking steaks and held him in his place with this simple promise. If he left, they ate his steak.

"It sounds loco, I know, but I got a bridle on it and climbed aboard. I didn't need a saddle. I shoved my toes back into a heavy layer of horn, like a plate protecting the creature's neck. The bridle slid up into its mouth with the bit set just behind the strangest looking teeth you ever did see. There wasn't a single tooth but an entire ridge of them."

"Like a turtle?" Kenyon frowned. "Turtles have dental plates, not teeth."

"That describes it. One of the men with me said I had to ride fast. My mount could chew through the steel bit in a few minutes. Well, sir, I settled down, got my lariat out and set to herding the small critters. That didn't work too well since they snapped and bit at the rope until there was nothing but a frayed end left. I used it more like a whip, and that worked just fine. I got fifty of them running for a box canyon. When I got them all herded in, the three men with me got up in the rocks and started an avalanche, pinning them in."

"So you won this rodeo by doin' what we do all the time? You ever try to get a balky calf to move? You ever faced a stampede of a thousand scared beeves?"

Crow was lost in his story and took no notice of which cowboy spoke.

"I had to do more. The other three mounted up, on creatures like mine, and we lumbered out into a meadow. My mount didn't seem to move fast, but he damned near flew once he set his mind to it. Trouble was, turning him was almost impossible. How do you turn an arrow once it's in flight?"

Crow stared into the fire. The dancing flames formed creatures unlike anything he had ever seen, yet strangely resembling them in the way they shifted and moved with sinuous grace.

"The others kept pace. Then I saw what we had to bulldog. It was as big as our mounts, but it had three horns and a protective plate running from one side of its head to another. The damned thing was close to twenty feet long and had a tail with a spike on the end. One whack of that and I'd've been history. Like two of the others. They tried to bulldog it. One got gored and the other ended up impaled by that spiky tail. No bull has a stronger neck or moves that fast. Not one."

"So what did you do?" Flaco pulled his feet under his chair so he could lean closer to hear over the crackling fire.

"I got my mount running alongside, dug my boots into the side and then launched myself. I wrapped my arms around the two outer horns. The one smack on the tip of its nose didn't matter as long as I held onto the other horns. With them I used leverage to twist its head about."

"A good jerk will bring a doggie off its feet."

"This wasn't a calf. Hell, it was ten times the size of a bull. I used my weight and I used my strength, I dug in my boot heels and tore up a stretch of meadow for twenty feet or better. Then I got better leverage and heaved. It would have busted any rodeo bull's neck. As it was, I only flopped it onto its side. There was no way I could let up to hogtie it."

"So you let it go?" Slaughter frowned, trying to imagine the size of the gargantuan creature. It was too much for his limited imagination.

"The remaining man came to my aid. He looped all the rope he had around a hind leg. Almost got smashed by the tail. Then he secured a front foot--the opposite to the one in back. That kept it down, but from the way it thrashed about, it would drive one of those horns clean through me if I let go."

"What did you do?" Kenyon scooted closer to hear over the rising wind.

"My arms got tired mighty fast. I strained so much it ripped my shirt across my shoulders." To show what he meant, Crow reached out and tensed. The cowboys' eyes grew big when they saw the thick slabs of muscle and how he strained the seams of his shirt.

"I couldn't hang on any longer, and the other man wasn't able to help. The left horn caught me in the gut, lifted me and tossed me about like I was a rag doll."

"What did you do then? Die?" Slaughter wasn't buying any of it now.

"Tried to hold my guts in. I hadn't noticed before but the others had started a fire and had a branding iron in it. On hands and knees, I got to the fire, took the iron and used it to burn shut my wound."

"You branded yourself?" Slaughter laughed now.

"Something like that. Then I branded the hind quarters of that hogtied monster before letting him go. A Circle C brand. Turned out there were a half dozen more to brand in that valley. I stayed there for another week, tracking them down and branding their haunches, me and the remaining cowboy." He heaved a deep sigh. "That first one taught me how to bring one down and I figured out how to escape getting gored again. The worst was a critter that lived off the ones we branded. It stood taller than any building I ever did see, had tiny arms but a mouth full of more teeth than there are stars in the night sky."

"This wasn't no rodeo," Slaughter said. "This was a roundup. You were branding those things, not competing for a prize."

"I suppose you're right. It was a roundup."

"Why'd you brand them? Was there some rancher up in the valley?"

"Turned out there was. He paid me ten pounds of gold and offered a part ownership in his herd for the work I did. He was an all right fellow, but there were others in the valley that weren't. One ugly son of a bitch ran his clan from higher in the hills. We came to something of an understanding. Any carrying a brand were ours. The mavericks were good for him and his people."

"It sounds like one of them horny critters would feed an entire town," Kenyon said.

"He led twenty or thirty people. All he needed was one every week or two. That let the owner of the Circle C grow his herd to a couple hundred, but he finally had to call it quits. Finding men to wrangle was too hard. He let the stock run free and moved on to where life was easier."

"That left the critters to the clan? You went and left everything to some crazy religious guy? I heard tell of entire towns down south and over in Utah that believe the craziest things you ever did hear," Flaco said. "Why some places, they have one man with a dozen wives. That's not for me, no sir. Keeping one woman satisfied is work enough."

"For you it would be. Not for me and Kenyon." Slaughter looked smug at his insult.

The joking went around the table. Crow leaned back, rubbed his belly and took a deep whiff. The steaks were almost ready.

"You gents get ready for the best meat you ever swallowed."

Crow pushed back and went to the grill. He flipped over the steaks to get a golden brown on them. The cooking odor made him rub his own belly again, but not so much because he was hungry. He pulled up his shirt and studied the Circle C brand there that had burned shut the nasty wound put into him by the three-horned monster. Saying the owner of the Circle C had long since gone would keep the three cowboys from trying to find that valley, but Crow knew they would never get up the

10

curiosity to do any exploring. They weren't the kind to wonder where lightning came from or why the stars burned at night or if herds of monsters filled a hidden valley.

"Hurry up with them steaks, Crow. I may be scrawny looking, but I got an appetite twice either of them." Kenyon slid closer to the table.

"Coming right up." Crow carried all three plates out, set them down and then added silverware.

It didn't take any prodding for the men to dig into their meal. They gobbled up the steaks until only the shiny plates remained, along with a few bones.

Flaco leaned back and groaned.

"That was one fine piece of meat. Almost as good as Pecos beef."

"Almost? Better," insisted Kenyon. "I can do with another."

"You finish it, I'll give it to you for free," Crow said. He returned to the grill and opened the small cooler where he kept the steaks. The top one still carried a Circle C brand, but Kenyon would never notice when the meat was properly seared.

Crow flopped the meat onto the plate, the Circle C brand down so it wouldn't show. The cowboy forked in one succulent piece after another until most men would have exploded. He finally finished.

"That don't taste like beef, but it's good. Tender, juicy and just the thing I needed to fill my empty belly."

"Glad you liked it," Crow said. "And that second steak is on the house. I'm always glad to see a man with an appetite."

"Jesse didn't steer us wrong. Good food." The three stood, fished out coins and crumpled greenbacks to pay, went to the door, opened it cautiously to the harsh wind and quickly discussed their chances of getting back to their ranch before the weather made travel too dangerous. Wyoming wind cut through a man's flesh like a razor this time of the year.

"We'll be back, Crow," Flaco said.

"Get some manners, you lout," Kenyon said. "Any man

who serves beef--"

"Meat," Crow corrected.

"Anyone serving up meat that good deserves some respect. What's your name? Your full name?"

"Crow's good enough, but the last name's Magnin."

"You get more of those steaks for when we come back to town, Mr. Magnin. I'll bring the rest of the hands from the ranch, and we'll eat you out of house and home," Kenyon promised.

Crow watched them hang onto their hats as the wind tried to whip them from their heads. The trio mounted and began the cold trip back to the Triple D. He rubbed the scar on his belly thoughtfully and knew he had to make a trip into the hills to slaughter another of the Circle C herd before the cowboys returned. With appetites like theirs, an entire triceratops might not be enough.

BLOODHOUND

C. COURTNEY JOYNER

The footfall was light and delicate. It barely touched the ground. But Jim Bishop heard it; damn the devil's eyes, he heard it, he surely had. Jim steadied the Henry rifle against his bloody shoulder, letting the barrel search from outcrop to outcrop. He thought he saw something move in the shadows that butted against the light blue of the August moon. He thought...

Jim sipped the last drops from his water bag, but his mouth still felt like sandpaper. He'd been on this manhunt for five straight days and each one was worse than the last.

He'd started hot and eager, reading vague moccasin scuffs that led to a barranca under sharp limestone cliffs. Jim spent day two belly-crawling through the underbrush and eyeing horse biscuits. The hardening crust told him he was at least ten hours behind the mare and her outlaw rider, but he'd close their lead if he could keep up the pace. His prey was running like hell, so he had to run too.

The third day, a sidewinder spooked his pinto. The horse reared back and stepped hard into a prairie dog hole, snapping its left flank. The leg broke clean so Jim killed him clean, putting a single .44 slug behind the ear. He wiped his tears, and asked the open sky for forgiveness to feel better about killing his horse, but it didn't ease him none.

Days four and five saw Jim running hard on swollen feet, searching for his man from dawn until the sky started bleeding in the west.

Now Jim was bleeding too, and he didn't want to think about how much blood he'd lost. Squirreled against the rocks, he tried to ignore the red stream inching down his side. Hell, Sheriff Gus Beaudine took half a load of buckshot from a Greener to his guts, and still rode down on a gang of mail robbers and killed all three. That's what Gus always bragged, and if the old man could do that, then Jim figured he could bite through the pain that ripped at him now. Jim had a badge on his chest just like old Gus. Didn't that mean he was a damn tough lawman too? Wasn't that why Gus deputized him?

Questions swirled through Jim's mind, and he started to drift. His own breath and heartbeat offered comfort. They were there. Barely. But it was the sudden jolts of pain that reminded Jim he was still alive, which was more than could be said for the cot girl from Hondo. She was the deadest thing Jim had ever seen. Her crinolines and flesh were shredded, so Jim couldn't tell skin from cloth, or raw muscle from store-bought finery. Jim wanted her one-eyed face out of his memory, but she wouldn't budge. Her specter reminded Jim why he was here, and that he had to hang on, even with his life sticky on his fingers.

Jim's eyelids got heavy again. Behind them, he was sweeping out the two rusty jail cells and Sheriff Gus Beaudine was hollering, "Get out here, boy! I got somethin' real sweet for ya!"

Jim's breath caught in his throat and his knees wobbled with excitement as he charged from the cells and then stood at silly attention before the Sheriff's desk, arms cradling a broom like it was a Winchester.

Beaudine licked the last brown drop of breakfast bourbon from his bristle and squint-eyed Jim. "Boy, you're always cryin' about how you don't get to prove yo'self. Well, how'd you like to track me a killer?"

Jim tossed the broom and grinned wide as Beaudine pulled a bent tin star from the drawer and handed it to him. "You're already out the door and ya don't even know what I want done. Calm down, pin that on, and swear to uphold the law."

"I-I s-swear, sir" Jim said, pricking his finger on the back of the star. With the badge on his shirt, Jim snapped back to attention like he thought a good deputy should.

"Now if ya have to shoot somebody, there won't be hell to pay. You know anythin' about that Cowboy Paradise?"

Jim nodded. "I've heard some things, but I've never been."

"Well, Rayford's the fella who runs it, and he's a good … citizen. Takes care of folks. His best girl got butchered by some crazy sum'bitch and he wants his head." Beaudine looked out his barred window to the middle of the street where a pair of yellow dogs were tearing into each other. "I'll settle for the bastard markin' time in Yuma, but if ya have to kill him, go ahead and do it."

"I-I've never been so proud, I mean, y-you really think I can bring this murderer in?"

"I'm sendin' ya, ain't I? Get out there. Rayford'll give ya the details. Take one of the Henrys and a box of cartridges."

Jim pulled the rifle from the rack and checked the action. "Sheriff, I can't thank you enough for showing faith in me. And I promise I'll honor the badge. A fugitive who thinks he can outrun me, well sir, let me tell you—"

"I've heard it all before." Beaudine belched then poured his fourth Rosebud of the day. "You swear you can track a man better than a bloodhound. So go an' prove it. And don't make me look a damn fool."

The whiskey-soaked Sheriff vanished from behind Jim's eyes as a fire of pain tore through his insides. The burning started low, then raced along the edge of his open wounds. Jim stuffed his fist in his mouth to stop from screaming. He wouldn't give away his position. No way. The fire eased as Jim huddled against the rock face, keeping his rifle low, so the moonlight couldn't dance off the barrel and show him up. He fingered the tin star. If he was going to die, then he'd take the crazy he'd tracked down with him, and that meant getting the killing shot. No matter what, this deputy was going to have his chance, and bring his prey down.

Jim tried to figure what he'd say to God. He knew he'd have to explain a few things, but at least he'd started this journey clean, wanting only to track his man and make a good job of it. He thought a capture was as good as a kill, but not anymore. Not after seeing what he'd seen inside Cowboy Paradise. God would understand that the animal that had done that violence had to be stopped cold. Yes sir, He'd understand.

The thought made Jim smile. His finger relaxed on the trigger. He felt like he had a sacred mission now, and anything he did was justified. If Noll Rayford could hear Jim say that, it'd be sweet music to his cauliflower ears. Jim didn't like Rayford at all, but now he and the flesh peddler had something in common.

The memory replayed easily for Jim: he was still a quarter of a mile away when Rayford began waving and shouting, his Dublin brogue boiling over. "You're the law? Gus leeches a hundred a month from me, and when I've got troubles he can't even come himself? Boy-o, you don't look old enough to shave!"

"Well, the Sheriff of this county thinks I'm old enough to get the job done."

Jim dropped from the pinto. The horse nosed a water bucket hanging from the back of Cowboy Paradise. He drew his rifle from its leather shoe and took in "Paradise:" a wind-beaten prairie schooner with a purple bonnet and gold tassels fringing its sides. The wagon sat in a dry creek bed surrounded by acres of scrub that led to the foothills and then the mountains beyond. Some yards off, a red mule lazed in the shade next to Rayford's bedroll and coffeepot. Jim hid his surprise; he'd heard that men who traded in sin lived better than this.

Rayford bit the end off an unlit cigarillo. "I want one of them stakeout deals where the ants eat the killer's eyes, know what I'm talking about?"

Jim's response was a neutral shrug as he looked under the wagon at a crude faro table, a worm-eaten bathtub, and a tower of filthy shot glasses. After a month on the trail, Paradise would look damn sweet to a saddle-sore cowhand, eager to spend his pay. That's what Rayford was selling and he probably still had every dollar that ever crossed his sweaty palm.

The pimp grabbed Jim and spun him around. "You gotta send the right message! Bury that howling buck up to his neck and let the other Apaches see it! They understand that kind of punishment—treatin' them like they'd treat any white woman if ya gave 'em half the chance."

"You mean a Red Man hurt the lady who works for you?"

"A Red—? Sweet Christ on a crutch! Didn't Gus tell ya nothing? That wild one whose Pa is some kind of horseshit medicine man, he done it. Claims to be a cousin to Geronimo. When he came out of them hills looking for Stella, I should'a shot him on the spot. Nobody woulda blamed me!"

"Then you knew he was trouble?"

"Yeah. But he was a customer. So what?"

"Sir, it's illegal to sell whiskey to Indians."

Rayford poked Jim's chest with a stubby finger. "You better be kidding. Don't turn this around on me. I'm out a good whore! Maybe she was only worth fifty cents a ride, but she was mine! And she didn't deserve what she got. Take a look, boy-o. Stella's not going nowhere."

Jim climbed the whiskey-crate steps up to the wagon tailgate, parted the canvas cover and peered inside. Rayford laughed as Jim reeled, trying to steady himself with the rifle, while fighting to keep his breakfast down.

The pimp settled on the bottom crate. "There's your noble savage for ya."

Jim was still doubled-over. "H-How? Did you see?"

"He must've had a long blade in his leathers." Rayford's

18

words were flat but protested any responsibility. "I didn't see a damn thing! He paid and went in. I poured a hot cup and checked me money box. She didn't even yell. Apaches are pretty good at that, killing without making a sound. I hollered when his time was up, but he was long gone and she was like, well, what you saw."

Jim hefted himself onto his saddle, cradling the Henry .44. "You don't know me, Mr. Rayford, but I'm a true bloodhound. I can track this man. And I'll bring him in for trial."

"What the hell are you going on about? No Apache gives a damn about white man's law, and I'm still out a whore! I've got to bury what's left of Stella, wash down the wagon, and find me another crib girl who'll work this trail! I'm owed for all that! I want to see his head, ya hear me? I'm owed!"

Rayford kept bellowing, but Jim already had his pinto at a full gallop, pushing the little horse as hard as he could to get away from the fat man's words. Stella's mouth and tongue were gone but she was crying louder than Rayford ever could. That's what Jim was hearing as he snapped the reins, angling his horse toward a wide thicket.

Jim eased to a walk and eyed the dry scrub. There were two fresh breaks in the tangle and the sun-browned grass had been flattened by someone falling. Jim could make out footprints in the loose dirt, but they were as indistinct as ghosts. No toes, only heel. He thought his quarry was wearing moccasins, which meant the rocks wouldn't slow him down. The bloodhound allowed himself to smile; he had the scent and he could follow it. He was doing all right. That was the first day.

Jim Bishop's mind snapped back to the present: it was now the fifth night and he was dying. The West Texas wind cut deep into him as he pulled his jacket tight with his one good hand. He was as ready as he'd ever be for another attack, provided it came while he could still see, and had the strength to pull a trigger. Sure. No problem at all.

Less than an hour before, Jim was chasing a figure over the rocks. He had the scent and was closing in. Jim dropped into a granite V, took aim, and split the dark with two shots from the

Henry. He missed, but the orange muzzle flashes illuminated his target; a young Apache brave who moved faster than any man Jim had ever seen.

Their eyes met for a moment before the brave leapt for an overhang, grabbed it with his fingers and swung easily on top of a steep rock face. He was gone before Jim could even draw a bead.

Feet slipping on gravel, Jim scrambled for a better position. He reached out to grab a twisted root above the entrance of a small cave, pulling himself onto a narrow ledge that ran the width of the cave's mouth. Jim perched and listened for his prey. Something moved, and he whipped his rifle toward a grey bat, fluttering in the shadows. The thing screeched past the deputy, laughing at him as it spun into the night sky.

Jim let out his breath, but he didn't relax. The Apache was close and Jim's nerves were electric under his skin. He detected something in the slight breeze that almost made him shoot. Almost. But Jim didn't want to show-up his position again. Still scared as hell, Jim's thoughts were clear: he'd blood-hounded the killer this far, and wasn't going to lose the Apache by being over eager. He'd vowed to bring his man in and that's what he was going to do, just like he told Gus he would. No brag, just fact.

Jim's side had opened so fast he didn't even feel it.

A sharp edge sliced through his skin, skidded along his ribs and was gone. Red blurred Jim's eyes, blinding him as the edge cut him again, ripping his shoulder and right arm to the bone. Jim rolled, jammed the rifle into the attacker and fired point-blank. As the gun-smoke cleared, he wiped the blood from his eyes and struggled to fire again.

He did. But his attacker was gone.

Jim lay dying, his mind washing in the memory of how he got here. Everything he did led him to this spot. He had a good position in the rocks, twelve shots in the magazine, plenty more in his ammo box, and a pool of blood spreading from his gut. It wasn't right. The deputy shouldn't be the one who was slipping away, and Jim kept whispering to himself that he was going to get his man. He couldn't stand, but he was going to catch a killer. Nice thought. Another bolt of pain reminded Jim that he wasn't going anywhere, and he curled up on his wet side, listening to his own shallow breathing.

"God," Jim said, "You know I ain't never done nothing like this before in my whole life; I don't know what the hell I'm doing out here. I ain't no tracker, I'm just a sorry bullshitter, and I don't blame ya if you let me die—"

A wood-smoke-smelling hand clamped over Jim's mouth, killing his private talk.

"I am Whistle Fire," a voice whispered in Jim's ear. "I am here to save you. Do not make a sound."

Jim nodded and Whistle Fire removed his hand. Jim didn't cry out. It took all his strength to draw his next series of breaths, while he fought to focus on the figure before him. The full moon's light showed Jim a massive silhouette, shoulders crowned with bearskin and the teeth of mountain lions shone around his neck and wrists. A large silver cross centered on his chest and captured broken pieces of Jim's own reflection.

Whistle Fire's voice was deep and quiet, "Lay down your gun, Deputy."

Jim held the rifle tight.

Whistle Fire stared into Jim's eyes. "You have not lost your mind. I am Apache, and I know your language. Some of us do."

"I know them b-beads and I kn-kn-know them colors. You gonna finish me off?"

"If you know that, then you know I am medicine. I can't help you while you keep your arms like that. Lay down the rifle."

Whistle Fire pulled a soft hide bundle from his belt and opened it. Jim watched him as he laid out his implements: Fire cut a peyote bud in half and threaded a needle with thin, stretched gut. His moves were sure and he didn't look at the deputy once. "If I wanted to kill you, I could have four sunrises ago. Why are you doing this? You're just a boy. Your life should end in a soft bed many years from now, surrounded by your children."

Before Jim could speak, Whistle Fire forced the peyote into his mouth and clenched his jaw. Jim bit into the bud. The dry plant broke apart and its bitterness made him gag.

"Let the taste fill your mouth," Whistle Fire said, "then swallow. Do not think of anything."

The pieces stuck to the roof and sides of Jim's mouth, drinking the last bit of moisture there. Jim chewed the bud, and his grip relaxed as the mescaline traveled warm down his back and arms, carrying him away. The feeling wasn't like being drunk on Old Kentuck, or anything Jim had known before.

"You cannot kill him," Whistle Fire said and took the Henry.

Jim grabbed at the shadow of a root, thinking it was his rifle. "It's my duty…you don't know… what he's… done…"

Whistle Fire wiped the blood from Jim's side. His words were flat. "He has shamed my people. He has lain with white women and traded hides for whiskey. He kills for pleasure. This is not right."

"Sure ain't, Whistle F-Fire… That's why… I…"

"I know better than you. A white man cannot kill him."

Jim's words slurred. "I have to…"

"You have never killed a man."

"Never shot nothing but a jack rabbit…but I told everybody in town I could bring him in…dead or alive…I told 'em 'cause I got a way of findin' a man…I'm a blood— bloodhound."

"You do not hear what I say. You cannot do any of these things."

"But I gotta …"

Below the two men, a shadowy shape moved silently from the mouth of the cave, along the edge of the drop-off, to a foothold. It darted up the side of the rock face, moving quickly hand-over-hand. It stopped at a place where it could watch Jim and Whistle Fire. Just watch.

The needle pierced Jim's flesh. He smiled as Whistle Fire laced the wound, laying muscle against bone and cleaning it with root poultice. "Who sent you? That fat Sheriff?"

"Old Gus is the law…"

Whistle Fire snorted. "He is a drunken coward who sent you because he knew he would not survive. I watched you track. You lost your horse, your water. But you didn't stop. You followed into these hills when others would have quit. You did your duty as an Apache would. Be proud of that."

"See…that's why they call me bloodhound."

"Who calls you that?

Jim swallowed quietly, "Well, only me…"

Jim stayed on the hazy, warm edge. The pain was somewhere out of reach now, in another existence, and the truth kept tumbling out. "I've never done no real tracking before. Just read about it, and played cards with a scout from Fort Smith who told me some things. You think I'm lyin' but I got a sense; I know when there's blood in the air. Or fear. Fear sweats right out of a man, and I can follow him. That makes me a bloodhound and an honest-to-God deputy, see that badge?"

Whistle Fire pulled the last stitch. "What did you do to earn it?"

"I sweep the cells. Clean the rifles. Once I put a summons in a guy's pocket while he was sleeping. And the Sheriff sends me across the street when he needs a re-fill…" Jim struggled to stand. "Maybe I ain't the world's best lawman, but I still got something to do …"

"No you don't." The medicine man opened the magazine and laboriously jacked each remaining cartridge from of the Henry, letting them drop to the ground. The brass hit the rocks like a gentle rain.

Jim drew a deep breath. "He's here..."

And then an enraged animal's scream split the air. The shadowy shape leapt on Whistle Fire and pounded his head against the sharp stones of the outcrop. Red sprayed like a fountain from the medicine man's temple as he brought his knees up against the thing's chest, pushing it off with a burst of raw strength.

Jim lurched forward, trying to fight. To help. But his mind reeled. Was he seeing a peyote dream? Narrowed red eyes lanced him, but they seemed like distant stars. Time slowed as Jim grabbed the rifle and swung it wildly into line. He eared back the hammer and pulled the trigger. It clicked on an empty chamber as the deadly shape moved on him. Jim felt his heartbeat, but little else. He fell out of his body and watched it being torn, and could not prevent it. Teeth sliced Jim's face. Hot saliva soaked him. Long claws ripped his stitches apart. Jim's nostrils were filled with the familiar pungent scent—the scent he'd followed these five days. Then pain erupted again, squashing the effects of the peyote. Jim rag-dolled to the ground.

The medicine man took his bone-handled knife and swiped the blade across his temple, smearing it with his own blood.

Jim straightened to his knees and battled as best her could, reaching up and digging his fingers into what he hoped were the creature's eyes, or the flesh of its throat. The deputy screamed; he was nothing more than a prairie dog being shaken to death in the jaws of an enormous wolf.

Everything was spinning when Jim saw Whistle Fire climb a small ledge and jump onto the thing's back. The medicine man plunged the knife blade into the shapeshifter over and over. The shoulders. The arms. The neck. The thing twisted. A cry exploded from its open maw. The cry didn't stop as it thrashed, but gradually it transformed from something guttural to something human.

A young man's voice.

Whistle Fire spiraled away and landed hard. The knife remained buried to the hilt in the thing's shoulder. The Apache medicine man caught his breath, as the thing's flesh folded in on itself, its bones shifting and muscles snaking into a different form . The long arms shortened and the lupine legs thickened at the calf. Silver hair receded under the taut, brown skin of a young Apache.

Tears glinted in Whistle Fire eyes as he watched human jaw and eyes settle into place. The snout-like nose collapsed, revealing the noble one underneath. Blood trailed across his naked body, but his face was peaceful. Dignified.

"I don't know what happened..." Jim mumbled. "I don't know what I'm seeing..."

Whistle Fire's lungs heaved. "Ba'cho." He looked at Jim and found the words.

"It means wolf. My son. Shape-shifter. Had you shot him a thousand times, he would not die. Only his father's hand could kill him. Our gods decreed it and so it is." His voice trailed off.

"Your son? I'm sorry..." Jim groaned.

"You will not die," the medicine man said. "I will see to that."

Jim was trying to take it all in, "So this is real...?"

"You'd take comfort if you'd been shot to pieces. That you can understand."

"I knew I was dying...that's how I fought back..."

"I said you will live. In town, you'll show your scars, but no one will believe your words. That is good. People will laugh at you, then forget everything. You will have dreams, but one day they will stop. Your life will go on, in another town, without a badge... But still, you will catch the scent when the need arises again. That is your duty, your curse."

Whistle Fire knelt beside his son's body. "There must always be a kill when the hunter finds its prey. Man, animal or both. If it was not my son, it would be you. You do not know what is out here. Beaudine did not know you were a bloodhound. He thought you were a lamb to be slaughtered."

Jim closed his eyes. "Maybe that's all I am." A sob came from his gut and Jim waited for the curtain to close on his mind. Something like sleep overcame him, and he let it happen.

The first touch of sun wasn't warm, but the light forced Jim's eyes open. Clean bandages wrapped his arms, chest and neck, and dried leaves marked the cuts on his hands and legs. Nearby, a barebacked chestnut nickered as if waiting for him. Whistle Fire was gone.

The rocks were spattered with dark brown stains that the rains would eventually wash away. There was a single, deep footprint made by a man carrying something very heavy. The bloodhound didn't follow that scent. Instead, he looked beyond it to the open land below him, and saw a jack rabbit darting through the scrub.

Nothing else moved.

Deputy Bishop wiped his wet eyes. He yanked the star from his shirt and let it drop. The bent blood-smeared tin clattered down a crevice and was lost.

The scent remained.

ROSIE'S CHICKEN & WAFFLES

EL CUCHILLO

Zeke had seen all manner of nature's savagery during a lifetime on the trails—death and dismemberment, cannibalism, all manner of killing—this was different. These were no bloody wolves, no mountain lions, no coyotes eating their own dead, no giant Tenochtitlan eagles sweeping down on the cool night breeze to carry off a tup or two. These were goddamn monsters from hell.

Q was twisted up, long legs stretching out with his boot heels in the dust, body low to the ground and his shoulder up against the edge of the trunk that was shielding them. Q had grown up hunting cougars in West Texas. He knew how to creep out, get a clear shot at a rabid heap of teeth and claws. Rosie called Q *Ol' Dog* and Zeke was the *Young Pup*. The Ol' Dog had hunted damn near everything that could be killed with a knife or a gun, but he didn't look like a hunter now. Zeke could feel Q next to him, trembling like an autumn leaf, the oaty smell of fresh piss wafting up to mingle with the stench of slaughter.

He ain't never shot no Chupacabra, Zeke thought. He remembered Rosie saying it, crossing herself over those big, sweet caramel teats and mumbling in her queer backwoods Spanish. Chupacabra. Goat-suckers. Demon Dogs.

The things had fallen on them quicker than anything Zeke had ever seen. They came dive-bombing out of the black night like eagles, but bigger. Black and huge and hungry. Goddamn panthers with wings. They came with an unearthly banshee howl and the sound of thunder behind them, picking animals from the ground with hooked talons and muscular arms, dropping them from high, the sheep wailing through the darkness as they plummeted back down to the rocky earth to burst like sloppy meat piñatas. Zeke had dropped to his knees, hands over his ears as livestock exploded around them like mortar shells. Q was half deaf already and still ducked his head, his face twisted up with the agony of the shrill blast of noise. The things had already picked off a half-dozen animals before either of the men had time to open their mouths in surprise. Zeke had screamed, and felt a rush of warmth down the front of his legs, when Ol' Dogs hand hooked in the back of his collar and yanked Young Pup from the dust, scrambling for cover behind the rotting hulk of a fallen tree. Now Zeke was clear-headed and Q was the one cowering in the dust.

Zeke pulled himself up and steeled his resolve to look out on what had turned a hard old cowboy like Q into a scared child. He thought better of it, remembering Rosie's stories of the dreaded goat-suckers. Twisted alien monsters that would just as soon gut a man as blink an evil, night-red eye. Creatures of the pit she'd called them.

Zeke looked at Q— body still as stone, hard and unforgiving— but his lips twitching like a hell-bitten dog. There was no reason left in the Ol' Dogs pale blue eyes, just panic.

Ought to leave him here, Zeke thought. *I ain't dying here. I can take care of Rosie. Rosie and her big warm tits, and those thick ruby lips. I can't carry the old bastard outta here, can I? Won't be my damn fault he lost his nerve. He's old and weak and...goddammit...*

Zeke clambered to his knees, demons be damned, and grabbed Q rough by the shoulders and cocked his arm back to lay a slap across the old man's face.

"Fucksakes, Quentin! Snap out of it!"

Zeke's hand flew out in a wide arc, but found nothing but air and he tumbled forward, face down in the dirt. Zeke reached out to the darkness. There were no screams from Q. There were just his eyes, wide and white and mad with fear, fading into the black night on the rhythm of beating wings, leaving Zeke alone and trembling under the blood red moon.

Zeke felt his legs moving under him before his brain registered the thought to run. The muscles were knotted hard as his legs pumped and his vision shook, barreling out of the clearing towards the cover of the clutch of pines standing on the east side of the clearing. The confused screaming of the sheep and the high-pitched wail of the demon-beasts was a furious wind blowing at his back, but all Zeke could hear was his own heart pounding in his ears and the rush of air in and out of his throbbing chest. So close. So very close. Zeke reached out to grab the thick green salvation of the branches, and felt the world spin as his foot caught on a stump and he flew forward, crashing to the rough ground a bare couple of feet from safety.

Zeke sat up and froze, realizing how deadly silent the night had become. Hot, moist breath, reeking of blood and rot, played against the skin of his cheek. The corner of his eye registered a shape, dark and thick, and as he turned, the terrible pieces of his ill-digested glances came together like a horrifying puzzle. It had a long, grey face. Skin stretched tight over hard bones, thick brow shrouding glassy eyes of hellfire red. It had a flat snout, like a bat, and a mouth full of serrated teeth, jagged and horrible, yet dwarfed by the two long dog-teeth that curved inwards of the gaping maw of the thing. Zeke felt another one moving in on his left. It nuzzled its snout into his neck, sniffing, and Zeke jerked away, causing the monsters to jump back, snapping in panic. There were three of them, half the height of a grown man, but twice as broad, and more heavily muscled than any thick-bred bull Zeke had ever seen. Zeke pulled himself into a crouch and began backing away from them, edging slowly toward the brush. It was a few short feet to the trees. The creature on the right jumped at him first, head shooting forward, long arms waving through the air, fleshy cape pulled flat against it, lunging with one sharp talon, flailing at Zeke's face. Zeke ducked and lashed out a boot that caught the thing full in the side of the head, knocking it back in the dirt with a squeal. It was only stunned for a second before jumping into the air with a whip-crack of its wings to disappear into the shadows. The other two advanced, creeping forward with their awkward waddle, arms dragging behind them. Both bared their fangs and screeched, their voices combining to create a single ear-splitting sound that bored through Zeke's head and blinded his every sense. He rolled, desperately trying to crawl free of the clearing and bury himself in the thick wall of trees. Two feet. Just two feet. Zeke forced his hands away from his ears and reached out for the trees, shaky legs moving an inch at a time beneath him. The wail of the beasts was replaced by a high-pitched whine inside Zeke's ears and he put a hand to the side of his head, fingers coming away sticky and hot.

He didn't hear the thud as Ol' Dogs body exploded in front of him like an overstuffed garbage bag, blood and meat and god knows what else, spattering up into his face. There was no head and, perhaps worse yet, the torso was wide open and empty, like a gutted turkey in a torn denim shirt. Zeke could see the inside of the rib cage, little notches and chunks missing from the short ribs, where one of the damned things had taken a bite. Zeke felt his gorge rise up in his throat and a tight lump form in his chest. The meat-husk was wearing Ol' Dogs boots, the tooled leather ones, with the big letter 'Q' just above the ankles, the boots Rosie gave him for their anniversary last fall, just before she started taking Young Pup to her bed instead of the Ol' Dog.

The thought of Rosie brought Zeke to his senses. He stood and dove past the carcass of his oldest friend, rolled over his shoulder and took to his feet, tumbling into the hard scrabble of the underbrush, branches tearing at his shirt and his skin, and he'd never been so happy.

Safe, Zeke thought. *Need a goddamn coffee. Whiskey. Some of Rosie's good chicken and biscuits.*

The last thought lodged in his throat, with the sound of pine trunks cracking and a pressure at the base of his spine as one hooked talon sliced through his backbone and his face hit the dirt with no feeling.

Rosie? Rosie. No! I made it to the trees! Rosie?

He only felt the blood rush to his head as he was pulled up into the treetops, and he felt nothing more than wind in his eyes as the ocean of green and the hard ground below rushed back towards his face.

I'm comin' Rosie. I'm comin'! I made it to the...

THE GIFTS OF A FOLDING GIRL

SCOTT S. PHILLIPS

Curtis Deak and Ray Watkins were in some serious shit, there was no two ways about it. It'd all seemed pretty straightforward when they'd set out that morning—but the best laid plans and all that. Of course, they hadn't done a whole lot of what could really be called *planning*, and that may be where things started to go outta whack.

Curtis was big on planning, at least *after* a job, when he was drinking a whiskey and looking back on it. *Next time it'll be different*, that sort of thing. Never was, though, and now he and Ray were stuck in this dilapidated cabin somewhere the hell in northern New Mexico Territory with about twenty-eight dollars to show for their efforts and a posse of trigger-happy gunmen camped outside. That's what you get for shooting up the *second* most-popular saloon in town.

But *next* time, that one's for sure. He was gonna plan the ass-end out of *that* one.

"Sonofabitch," Ray said, cautiously peering out the window. "That's Ken Bingham out there with 'em."

"You sure?" Curtis stayed put on the cabin floor. He'd already gotten his ear nicked by a bullet when he risked a peek

34

a little earlier.

"Hell yeah I am—he's wearin' that stupid hat."

"Son of a bitch," Curtis said. They'd ridden with Ken and his fancy English hat, pulled some jobs with him—poorly planned ones, sure, but they had history. And now he's ridin' with the posse on their trail?

"What the hell they payin' you, Ken, you prissy shitheel?" Ray hollered.

"Six dollars," Ken yelled back.

Ray looked at Curtis. "Told ya it was Ken."

"Nothin' personal," Ken added.

"The hell it ain't," Curtis yelled from his spot on the floor. He waited for a reply but none came. "Can you see how many of 'em?"

Ray took another peek. "I ain't sure. Five, maybe."

Curtis looked around the cabin, a one-room affair with no back way out, except for a window too small to crawl through. "I got me an idea."

"I'm open to pretty much anything," Ray said. "But I ain't real inclined to rush 'em, if that's what you got in mind."

"Nothin' so bold as that." Curtis dug around in the pockets of his jacket, hoping he still had what he was looking for. "Remember that magic wagon rolled through town a few weeks back?"

"Yeah, they put on a pretty good show's I recall," Ray said. "Not sure I see how that's gonna help us outta this fix, though."

"I got somethin' from that Navajo girl—the one that folded herself up into that little box?"

"I'll bet you got somethin'," Ray said. "Crabs, no doubt."

Ignoring Ray, Curtis continued to dig. Wasn't in the outside pockets. Things might be dire. He opened his coat and fished through the pockets in the lining. "There we go," he said, pulling a small leather pouch tied up with a string woven from what looked like human hair.

"What ya got there?" Ray asked.

Curtis tossed the pouch up and down a couple times,

feeling its weight. "I caught that girl giving me the eye, and after the show was over, she come over to talk."

"How'd I miss this?"

"You'd gone off to the saloon by then. Anyway, this conversation we had got real innerestin', you take my meaning, and I guess I held up my end okay, because that girl decided to give me this here pouch as a gift afterwards."

"Hoo," Ray said, shoving his hat back on his head a little. "What's that Indian pussy like?"

"Never you mind the details, what's important is this here magical pouch."

"Magic—aw, son, that girl took ya. I hope you didn't pay her too much for that thing."

"I told you, I didn't pay her nothin', it was a gift for services rendered," Curtis said, offended. "And she done a demonstration for me so I'd know how to work it—I seen it with my own eyes, and it's magic, all right."

"An Indian thing?"

"Naw, she made a big point of sayin' it weren't Indian. She learnt it from another guy rode with the wagon for awhile, till a rattlesnake crawled into his bedroll with him one night."

"Didn't do that fella much good, I'd say."

"She called it somethin' in Navajo," Curtis said, struggling to remember. "Nish… *Nishhin 'aliil*, that was it. Said it means slippery magic or greasy magic, somethin' like that."

This time Ray lifted his hat clean off, scratched his head a little, then replaced the hat. "Well, we ain't got nothin' better to pin our hopes on, I suppose I'm willing to give the ol' slippery magic a chance."

"That's the spirit." Curtis looked around, settling on the kerchief tied around Ray's neck. "Lemme have that kerchief."

"That's my good one," Ray said.

"Good enough to dress up your corpse?"

Ray frowned. "All right." He untied the kerchief and handed it over. "You ain't gonna ruin it, are ya?"

"Naw," Curtis said. Getting to his knees—with a glance toward the window to make sure he wasn't providing a nice

36

target for one of the gunmen outside—he spread the kerchief flat on the floor in front of him. "Find me a rock or somethin'—somethin' heavy, about the size of an egg."

Staying low, Ray started skoonching around the cabin floor, looking for something suitable.

Curtis untied the pouch, cupping it in the palm of one hand as he opened it. Inside was a small mound of fine, white powder with just a hint of a sparkle to it in places. Carefully, Curtis shook some of the powder onto the kerchief, eyeballed it for a moment, then shook out a bit more. He folded up the pouch again, tied the string, and returned the pouch to his pocket.

Nosing around the fireplace, Ray found a wobbly chunk of stone in the hearth and started wiggling it back and forth like a loose tooth. "I think I got somethin'll work." He glanced back at Curtis, who was unbuttoning his pants. "Hey, what the hell are you up to," Ray said, frowning.

Curtis unslung his pecker and pointed it at the powder heaped in the center of Ray's kerchief. "Tryin' to work up a piss," he said.

"Not on my goddamn good kerchief you ain't," Ray said.

"Come on outta there now, you bastards," said a voice from outside.

Curtis looked at Ray. "You want, I can tuck this thing away and we can go on out."

Ray frowned. "I don't wanna do that, but I ain't clear on why you feel the need to piss on my kerchief, neither."

"It's part of the magic." Curtis looked down at his pecker.

"What happens if you're pee-shy?" Ray asked.

"Then I guess you'd better hope you ain't ass-deep in hired gunmen." Curtis strained a little. "Here we go." A squirt of urine splashed out onto Ray's good kerchief, soaking the powder. "Shit," Curtis said, aiming off to one side and letting the flow continue.

"Now we're holed up in a cabin full of piss," Ray said. "Very magical."

The flow of urine trickled away to nothing and Curtis gave

his pecker a few good shakes before putting it away and buttoning his pants. "Ain't that much, I pinched it off. Gimme that hunk a' rock."

Ray wrestled the small stone free from the hearth and tossed it to Curtis. "Good enough?" Ray asked.

Curtis jiggled the stone around in his hand for a moment. "Seems like." Carefully, he plunked the stone down in the center of the piss-damp kerchief. Then, head down, he closed his eyes and muttered something Ray couldn't make out.

"What's that y'say?"

"Quiet now," Curtis said. "I'm makin' my spell." He mumbled a few more words, then opened his eyes and stared down at the mess in front of him.

Ray watched, curious, but not wanting to interrupt the spell-casting business.

"All right then," Curtis finally said. Gingerly, he folded the kerchief around the stone and tied it up tight.

"I still think this is all a big joke that Navajo girl played on the white man," Ray said. "Pissin' everywhere and then stickin' your hands in it."

"I told ya I seen a demonstration, this shit works." Curtis picked up the bundle and looked at Ray. "How good are you a thrower?"

"Oh I see, now you want me to handle your pee-rag," Ray said.

"We gotta throw this thing and hit Ken with it for the spell to work," Curtis said. "And I ain't got much of an arm."

"I seen you shoot the ass off a bumblebee once —"

"Throwin' ain't the same as shootin' and you damn well know it," Curtis said. "Now do you want a chance at gettin' out of this mess or should we just surrender right now?"

Ray huffed a little. "That damn thing's drippin' piss." He locked eyes with Curtis for a few seconds, then poked his head up to look out the window again. "Dammit, I suppose I could hit that asshole if I had to."

"Atta boy," Curtis said. "You don't have to hit him in the head or nothin', you just gotta get this mix of piss and magic powder on him somewhere."

Sighing, Ray stuck his hand out. Curtis shuffled over to him and dropped the bundle into his palm with a wet slap. Ray's face went sour. "This sure as hell better work."

"You hit Ken with that thing, we're gonna see results, I guarantee," Curtis said.

Unconvinced, Ray sized up the situation. "I'm gonna have to stand up to get a good throw. That's also gonna make me a good target."

"I'll cover you," Curtis said.

His back against the wall, Ray stood up next to the window, then took another peek outside. A shot rang out, the bullet chunking into the outside wall of the cabin not far from Ray's face. He looked at Curtis. "All right, I got a bead on Ken's hat. Put a couple shots out there."

Curtis drew his pistol and checked the cylinder. "I only got three left."

"Shit," Ray said, a funny look on his face. "Don't matter anyway—I just realized, you start slingin' lead out there, they're all gonna duck."

Curtis got that same funny look on his own face. "I didn't even think of that."

They stared at each other for a moment, brains percolating but not coming up with anything useful. That whole *planning* problem again.

"Guess I'm just gonna have to hope they're all lousy shots," Ray finally said.

"Sorry," Curtis said. "I wish I was a better thrower."

"Let's just get it over with, I'm tired of standin' here with a handful of your piss."

Taking a deep breath, Ray tested the weight of the bundle one more time, then quickly stepped in front of the window, arm drawn back. Two or three gunshots immediately boomed out.

Ray hurled the bundle as hard as he could. As it left his hand, a slug punched into his palm and out the other side, spattering Ray's face and hat with blood. Howling in pain, he dropped down out of sight, clutching his wounded hand.

"Ow," someone outside said.

Curtis inched up to the window and risked a peek. He could see Ken, goofy hat still in place, rubbing his right shoulder and looking around in confusion.

"Looks like you got him," Curtis said. He grinned back at Ray.

"Don't mind me if I don't celebrate too much just yet," Ray said, wincing at the pain in his hand. "If I still had my goddamn good kerchief I could use it for a bandage."

"Jesus Christ, I'm sorry you got shot, but you sure got a thing for that kerchief."

Ray put pressure on the bleeding gunshot wound with his good hand. "Why don't you gimme your shirt for a bandage and we'll see who's got a thing for a thing."

Curtis glowered at him. "For God's sake," he finally said. Stuffing his gun back in its holster, he started unbuttoning his shirt.

Hushed voices from outside made Curtis pause, listening. "They're throwin' rocks must mean they're out of bullets," someone said. "We might could rush 'em."

Ray perked up. "Maybe you'd better put a shot or two out that window, keep 'em hunkered down."

Curtis stripped off his shirt and handed it to Ray. "Enough about the damn kerchief now, all right?" As Ray began wrapping the shirt around his injured hand, Curtis drew his gun again and fired off a careless shot in the general direction of the posse. "You'd best rethink things," he yelled out the window.

Outside, Ken spotted the bundle underneath some scrub and bent to retrieve it. "Looks like they wrapped some cloth around it," he said.

"Some kind of message, maybe," Deputy Coleman said.

Sheriff Atwater frowned at him, his bushy mustache nearly hiding the expression. "What message they need to throw out here wrapped around a rock when they could just shout?"

Ken retrieved the bundle and stared at it in the palm of his hand. "It's wet," he said. Hesitantly, he sniffed at it, then looked at the Sheriff. "I think it's piss."

"Maybe you ought should put it down then," Sheriff Atwater suggested.

Ken whipped the rock back at the cabin. "Sonsabitches, throwin' a piss-rock at me!" The rock clunked off the side of the cabin and rolled away.

"That'll show 'em," the Sheriff said.

Ken's eyes went funny. "Fuck," he said softly.

Then he raised his pistol and shot Sheriff Atwater in the face.

"Don't tell me my boudoir deeds ain't worth some bonafide magic," Curtis said, peeking around the edge of the window.

"God damn," Ray said. "Your piss-magic did that?"

There was an odd moment of quiet after Ken shot Sheriff Atwater, but about the time the body hit the ground, Ken started shooting again and the entire posse finally decided it might be a good idea to return fire.

Deputy Coleman took a round in the chest and tumbled over backwards, giving Ken a clean shot at one of the other gunmen. That fellow had time to say "Oop" before Ken's next shot hit him in the throat and he went down gurgling.

Oswald Drummond, owner of the saloon Curtis and Ray had robbed, managed to shoot Ken in the left shoulder. Ken shot Oswald twice in the gut, then his pistol's hammer fell on empty chambers. Calmly, Ken stepped over the Deputy's writhing body to retrieve Oswald's gun, then began shooting at the remaining members of the posse. One of those boys turned tail and ran like hell into the woods, while the others dove for cover, wildly popping shots in Ken's direction.

"This is the craziest damn thing I ever seen," Ray said. He and Curtis weren't even bothering to peek anymore, they just stood at the window openly gawking.

Ken walked over to the tree the last of the gunman was hiding behind and shot the man dead. He stared blankly down at the corpse for a moment, then bent to pick up the man's gun. He looked around, but there were no more targets.

Groaning in agony, Deputy Coleman pushed himself up to a sitting position, the front of his shirt drenched in blood. With a shaky hand, he drew a bead on Ken and pulled the trigger. Ken staggered, hat sailing away.

"Shot that prissy hat right off Ken's head," Ray said.

Curtis pointed. "Shot more'n that off his head."

Hatless, Ken turned to look at Deputy Coleman, revealing a large hole blown out of the left side of his head, his ear dangling by a flap of skin and chunks of brain matter sliding down his neck.

"That's for you, you cocksucker," Deputy Coleman said.

Ken sank to his knees and fell face-first into the dirt, pistol tumbling from his grip.

"So much for Ken Bingham and his stupid hat," Ray said. "Did he get all of 'em?"

Curtis's lips moved as he counted bodies. "I believe he did. That sumbitch Deputy's still kickin', but I'm guessing not for long."

"Hell, we can just walk on outta here then."

Curtis grinned at Ray. "Appears that way, don't it?"

"Hold up," Ray said. "What's this?"

Curtis turned to look out the window again.

Ken was still face down on the ground, but his right hand—his gun hand—was twitching.

"Just a little kick left in the corpse is all," Curtis said.

Ken's right arm began flopping around. Then the left. Spastically, Ken's arms worked themselves under his body and he struggled to push himself up.

"Bastard ain't dead," Ray said.

Ken made it to his hands and knees, blood and brains dribbling from the wound in his head. Awkwardly, he looked around, eyes settling on his gun where it lay a few yards away. He crawled toward it like a palsied baby, trailing gore.

"You shitheel," Deputy Coleman wheezed. "I killed you dead." Weakly, the Deputy aimed his pistol at Ken once more, firing a shot into the ground in front of him. Another pull of the trigger put the hammer down on an empty chamber.

Deputy Coleman sneered at his gun. "Ain't that just fine."

A fat dollop of brains fell out of Ken's head, landing in the dirt next to his gun as he fumbled to get a grip on it. His fingers closing on the pistol, Ken smiled crookedly.

Deputy Coleman watched as Ken raised the pistol and aimed at him. "Asshole," the Deputy said as the gun went off. The bullet hit Coleman in the chin, tore through his head, and blew a wad of skull and meat out the back.

"Surely that's gonna wrap things up," Curtis said.

Ray kept an eye on Ken, who was now wobbling to his feet. "What exactly *was* that piss-magic spell you did?"

Curtis was quiet for a long moment, a nervous look on his face as Ken's wobbly, bleeding noggin zeroed in on the cabin—in particular, the window where Curtis and Ray stared out at him. "I suggested ol' Ken start shooting and keep on shooting."

"Well," Ray said, "I didn't bang no magical folding Indian girl so what do I know, but maybe that was a poor choice of words."

Ken fired a shot at the cabin, the bullet zinging past Curtis's previously nicked ear and thunking into the wall behind him. Curtis jabbed his gun out the window and squeezed off a wild shot, the bullet kicking up dust near Ken's feet.

"Seems like shootin' him ain't gonna do much good, what with his brains falling out on his boots and him still comin'," Ray said.

"Maybe if we shoot him enough," Curtis said. Both men ducked as Ken fired again, splinters exploding from the window frame and peppering their faces.

Ray squeezed his gun-shot hand, still trying to staunch the flow of blood. "Whatta you got, one bullet left?"

"Yeah," Curtis said. "How many you got?"

Ray frowned. "I didn't say anything earlier because I didn't want to sour your mood, but I'm out completely. Been so since a few hours back."

A couple of clicks from outside got their attention. They swapped a look.

"That sound like what I think it sounded like?" Curtis said.

Ray cautiously poked his head up to take a look. Ken was still shuffling towards the cabin, pulling the trigger on his empty gun. "He's out."

Curtis stuck his head up alongside Ray's. "Time to run for it, then?"

"That's what I'm..." Ray's words trailed off. "Wait, what's he doing now?"

Ken stumbled off to the right, towards Deputy Lester's corpse. Crouching, he pulled the Deputy's gun from his hand and aimed at the window where Ray and Curtis's heads were visible. *Click.*

Ken eyeballed the gun, puzzled. Then, as if slowly remembering how folks did things, he looked the Deputy's corpse over, settling on the man's gun belt.

"Uh-oh," Ray said.

Ken fumbled a handful of shells from Coleman's belt and opened the cylinder on the pistol.

"We could run right now," Curtis said, as he and Ray watched Ken slide the bullets into the gun. "He seems pretty slow."

"He ain't had a reason to run yet, and I ain't gonna bet my life he can't do it," Ray said.

"Well what the hell do you think we ought to do, then?"

Another glob of brains slid out of Ken's head, landing with a wet splat on Deputy Coleman's face. Shoving the last bullet into the gun, Ken flipped the cylinder shut and looked towards the cabin again, eyes narrowing.

"I suggest you work up another squirt a' piss and come up with some magic that might make this asshole lay down and die," Ray said.

Ken stood, walking stiffly towards the cabin. "Shit, he ain't shootin'," Curtis said. "I think he knows he's got us cornered, he's just gonna walk on in here and pick us off." Holstering his pistol, Curtis scrambled away from the window and started unfastening his pants. "Close them goddamn shutters, willya?" Peeling off his undershirt, he frantically spread it on the floor.

Ray banged the shutters closed, taking one last peek as he did so. Ken was nearing the cabin, gun held out in front of him. Grunting against the pain in his wounded hand, Ray threw the bolt, locking the shutters down.

Curtis held his prick in one hand while he fumbled the pouch of magic powder from his pocket with the other. He paused for a second when they heard Ken's footsteps hit the porch. "Come take my gun and put that last bullet to use if he gets in."

Ray scurried over to Curtis, grabbing his pistol and leveling it towards the door, breathing heavy.

Curtis bit down on the string holding the pouch shut and pulled it loose, dumping some of the powder on the undershirt at his feet.

Ray and Curtis jumped as Ken slammed into the door, straining against the latch.

Curtis glared at his pecker. "Jesus Christ, you'd think it'd scare it outta me, but I can't get a dribble."

Ken put a shot through the door, apparently aiming where he thought Curtis's voice was coming from. Unfortunately, Ray was standing in the path, the bullet punching into his midsection.

"Oh my Christ," Ray said, toppling backwards over Curtis and landing face-up on the floor, gazing up at Curtis's prick. Groaning, he clutched his belly where the bullet had struck. "Don't you piss on me, God damn it."

Giving up on the door, Ken went to the window and banged on the shutters. Panicked, Curtis finally managed to start pissing, the stream of urine soaking the front of Ray's shirt.

"And here I always thought you was the smart one," Ray said.

The shutters gave way, swinging inwards so suddenly Ken nearly tumbled through the window.

"Not *us*, you brain-damaged shitsnake!" Curtis screamed, running towards the window and desperately trying to pee on Ken. "You ain't s'posed to shoot *us!*"

Ken emptied his gun into Curtis, sending him flopping onto his back, pissing into the air like a spouting whale. Weakly, Curtis flung the pouch of magic powder towards Ken, but it fell short and scattered across the cabin floor.

Standing calmly at the window, Ken watched as Curtis choked up blood and died. Then he turned his attention to Ray, who swore and hollered right up to the instant his life finally slipped away in a thick gurgle.

Turning away, Ken looked out at the bodies strewn around the field in front of the cabin. Like a marionette on tangled strings, he shuffled out amongst the corpses, head down, loose ear slapping wetly against his neck with every step.

Then he found it.

Bending, Ken picked up his fancy hat, dusted it off, and placed it atop his head. Something wasn't right, though. Ken tilted it this way and that, to no avail, then gave up, letting the hat settle at an odd angle on his shattered melon.

His head hurt real bad, to be honest, and his ears were ringing something fierce. Staring down at the bodies surrounding him, he tried to recall who they were and what in the hell he was doing standing in a field of corpses in the first place. Everything was too damn fuzzy, though, and *son of a bitch*, did his head hurt.

That ringing grew louder, drowning out everything else. Ken started walking in the direction he thought the town might be, but he had no real idea where he was going. Shit, for that matter, he couldn't even remember if his name really was *Ken*. Whoever he was, his head hurt like hell and his feet seemed very far away and something was shrieking in his ears, and there was only one thing he knew for sure.

He was gonna need more bullets.

YOU ARE THE BLOOD

GRADY COLE

Billy peers out from behind spread fingers, eyes watering at the fierce light of day. Even cut by tinted glass, and filtered through the black lace of the curtains, the sun is blinding. And warm. So warm.

"What are they doing now?" Drago grumbles from his dark corner near the bed. "Are they not ready yet?"

"I don't know what all they gotta do. Whyn't ya come and look for yourself. The light ain't gonna hurt you. It feels good."

"I am not afraid of the light, Billy."

"I never said you was. Just come and see it." The boy turns back to his vantage point, peeking through spaces to gather an idea of the action in the street.

"There's Rado!" Billy shouts, jabbing a finger into the glass, "He's lookin' tough. Don't worry. He's gonna win, for sure."

"I am not worried, damn you!"

The man in the street, tall and lithe, a cascade of auburn hair like fire all that is visible under a wide-brimmed hat. Thin fingers, usually bone-white, now covered in leather gloves, taper like gnarled branches, reaching from the cuffs of his long black duster. Three smaller figures, draped in black cloth from head to toe, faces and hands swaddled in cloth, not an inch of skin open to the sunlight. They fuss at Rado's periphery, administering prayers and shouting to the wind.

"He's gonna get him, alright. That stranger ain't got no chance."

"Has no chance, Billy. You sound foolish when you say it wrong."

Billy scowls into his own face, reflected in the glass.

"You're just sore, on account of being too chicken to come over here and see for yourself."

Drago moves fast, a blur in the watery edges of Billy's vision. Billy leaves the ground—flying—now folding into the mattress, air leaving his lungs in a burst of hot air as Drago comes down on top of him.

Billy winces, pulls his head back against the pillow, trying to minnow away, trapped beneath the iron-bar strength of Drago's arms. Hot tears sting his face as he damns his own name, silently praying, terrified of Drago's red eyes and his anger.

"Arm."

"No, Drago. Please."

"Arm!"

Drago hops up to sit, keeping a vice-grip on one arm, tugging to bring it to level, Billy with no choice but to follow, helpless to remove himself from Drago's punishment.

Drago looks down at the arm, softens his grip, caresses it with a long, terrible finger. Bone white and thin like a birch sapling, the nails like talons curling from their terminus. Drago runs those fingers across Billy's arm to trace the scars, themselves long, thin, white. Some are faded into the peach of his skin, barely visible. Fresher wounds still pink, wider and deeper.

Billy whimpers.

"Shhhhh. You should not say such things to me, Billy. Are we not friends? Compatriots? Have I not spared you? Every day you live is a day given you by me."

"Yes, Drago," Billy whispers, desperate to please.

"Yes?" Drago taunts, "Yes, what?"

"Yes. Master."

Billy pulls gingerly at his captured limb, hoping to avoid what comes next. Drago tightens his grip.

"Not this time, Billy." Drago snarls, "Arm!"

Billy squeezes his eyes shut, focuses on blocking out the pain. The terror.

It begins with a tickle, feeling Drago dragging his teeth across the length of the inside of his forearm, as he has done so many times before, teasing, playing.

Billy pleads again.

Drago pulls harder on the arm, more pressure this time, letting his cold breath play on the hairs of the arm, feeling the pulse beneath his lips, the tiniest capillary flush and full, brought to life by terror; his to own, to devour, to torture.

Deeper still, dragging his teeth through the layers of skin, feeling them peel away beneath him, the canals of sweet and salty red nectar coming slowly, ready to be licked or suckled, Billy trembling in his hands, heart beating faster and faster, muscles twitching of their own accord.

Billy pulls away again. Feeling the muscles cramp as his shoulder tenses against the flicker of Drago's tongue against his now-raw skin. A movement outside catches his eye, a voice calling in the street.

"Drago!" he shouts. "Drago! It's time!"

Drago runs his pointed tongue from Billy's elbow to his wrist, moaning softly as he laps the red oozing from the boy, before relenting and releasing his hold.

Billy falls to the floor with the momentum as he tears his arm free of its captor. He clamps his free hand to the wound.

Drago is dabbing his mouth now, smiling at the boy cowering. Now turning away in disgust.

"Here, fool. you're going to rot your arm, putting that dirty hand on it like that. Why must you be so foul?"

Drago's kerchief lands a foot away from Billy. The boy lurches forward to grab it, before hunkering back into his corner, even as Drago steps tentatively towards the shrouded window.

"There he is." Drago's voice is a specter, hushed and thick with shadows of fear.

Billy is up, the white rag turning pink where it is now tied around his arm.

Billy creeps forward, hesitating as he comes closer to his companion, his master.

"He don't look so bad." Billy grumbles.

"They say he has killed other Princes." Drago's voice cold.

"He ain't shit." Billy, moving closer, regaining his confidence, feeling the danger subside, Drago distracted by this stranger in the street.

Billy ducks under the curtain to get a closer look, no longer afraid of the light, face pressed to the glass of the window, cool against the warped tint, a haze of sepia between him and the street.

The man on the opposite side of the street turns to stare directly at him. Eyes lock. Billy sees it. Ignores it. Questions it in the back of his mind.

Drago is behind Billy, whispering "They say he is an Old One. One of The First, from across the Seas."

Billy, huffing, says it again. "He ain't shit. Rado'll take him out easy. Rado is gonna be King."

The Stranger is large, more squarely built than any of Drago's people. The Stranger is bulky beneath his large coat, which covers him from ears to feet. The brim of his hat droops as if it has recently been wet, pulling down to shade what isn't already covered. He has no acolytes to service him or call his name out to the daylight. He stands alone and stares across at Prince Rado, champion of the Nights Breed, the someday King.

"He ain't gonna win," Billy says once more. "'Course, if he did… you'd be the Prince."

Drago answers with cold breath, pressing his sharp teeth into the soft skin of Billy's exposed neck. "Shut your mouth," Drago snarls.

Billy is trembling, eyes closed against the shadow of his

own death behind him, when the call rings out.

The acolytes point to the sky, to the fiery glow of the sun, directly overhead. The one furthest from Billy sounds the bells with a wave towards the church tower. The peals of brass crash through the empty streets like strange thunder.

One.

Drago, caught off guard in the midst of his bullying, nipping Billy's neck, tasting the copper warmth of red again. He shudders at the thought of Billy filling his mouth. He is licking his lips when…

Two.

Billy squeals and drops away, back to the window, hand to his neck, feeling the sticky heat of his precious life.

Three.

Drago lunging, shoving Billy to one side. "Move, stupid!"

Four.

Billy is up on his knees next to his master, heeling at his side, peering out the window, waiting. Waiting for…

Five.

The black shrouded acolytes raise arms together. The bells stop. The silence is electric.

They call out into the street, across the red dirt to the Stranger where he stands like a statue. Their benediction echoes in the open air.

"You are the blood," they call, "That which flows from the Earth."

The Stranger simply nods his head. Rado keeps his head bowed in mute prayer. These are the words. The same words. Every night upon waking, every night when they broke the fast.

"From the Night. To feed. To Fulfil. To bathe us in the blessed light of Darkness," they continue.

"You are the blood, and the blood must flow."

The acolytes fall to their knees at Rado's side as his jacket and hat whirl free of his body. Rado is a blur of bone and muscle, a white ghost spinning through the air, his weapons flying in majestic synchronicity.

The boys watch, enrapt, aware of every mote of dust swimming between them and their hero. The hush of a hundred voices behind tinted windows on both sides of the street as the Night's Breed wait out the seconds with lightning rising in their chests, nails curled in clenched fists, red eyes wide despite the sun.

The Stranger rolls to one side as the Prince Rado's hand-spears splinter into the wall behind him. The Stranger's coat stays on, but flies open as he comes to his knees, revealing some devil contraption firing missiles that sing through the air and catch Rado with deadly force.

One. Two. Three.

One takes his shoulder, one in the leg, dropping him to his knees, the last through the throat with the sound of a steak hitting the plate. The bacon sizzle follows as he folds forward into the dirt, the dreaded sun taking him layer by layer as his flesh burns away into embers on the wind.

The acolytes scream and turn to run, each of them taken by a single shot from the Stranger.

Drago screams and covers his eyes.

Billy is so close to the window. He can see it. He is sure now.

The eyes. The Stranger's eyes. They're blue.

"He's... he's..."

Human!

The word rises up in a choir, being screeched all around him, fiendish wails from all the halls of the Night's Breed. Feet pounding on floorboards as they scramble away from the windows, away from the sun.

The Stranger looks towards the window, towards Billy. He has something in his hand, a stick? A tube? A scroll of some kind? It rolls to the wall and strikes with a thud. It seems to flicker at one end. Is it a candle? Billy is wondering at it still when Drago grips his arm and tears him away, throwing him across the room towards the door.

"Get me to my chambers, you fool!" he commands, screaming, face contorting as he unleashes the full madness of his terrible maw, jaw stretching, row upon row of knives inside.

Billy is thrown against the wall as the blast tears open the building where he had stood mere moment before. Drago flying through the air like a toy, like a doll. Glancing off of the bed post and leaving one arm behind him on the floor.

Billy coughs and waves the smoke away from his face, watching dumbfounded as the light, the sunlight, streaks in through the smoke, followed by a boot, and then another. Billy's eyes rising up from the floor to gaze in disbelief as the Stranger waves his weapon through the room.

The Stranger steps slowly into the room, kicking Drago's lost arm to one side, and aims the weapon at Billy before leaning in close and whispering into Billy's wide blue eyes.

"Run, kid."

Billy stares after, still wide-eyed, as the Stranger steps past him, strange metal jangling at the back of his heavy boots. The Stranger steps over Drago, and into the hall, and each time his weapon whistles it echoes, and ends with a cry and the sound of another body crumbling to the floor in embers.

Drago moans beside him, and Billy stands, wincing at the pain at the side of his neck, where Drago had bitten down on him.

"Billy, please," Drago whimpers. "Please."

Billy looks at the boy. Hardly a boy. One hundred years old but no different than Billy to the eye. A hundred years of death. It comes like a secret voice echoing in Billy's head.

Billy crouches closer, tempted to poke at the ragged stump where Drago's arm had been separated. It would grow back, he knew. There were precious few dangers to being a Prince of Night's Breed, but he would need blood. Billy's blood. Who else was left to serve him?

"Billy. Arm." Drago croaked weakly.

Billy scowls, stands and begins to back way, still listening for the whistling of the Stranger's weapon. He can hear the screams from all around him. There are more Strangers out there. More humans. Not cattle like Billy's people had been.

His mother, his father, his siblings… All devoured by the Breed, or turned into pets. Playthings. Snacks.

Billy feels the warmth of the sun at his back.

"Arm!" Drago shouts, coughing. Pierced in at least five places, but not thoroughly enough to burn. Billy feels the heat rise up in him, a fury he has never known before. Humans. Real humans. Here.

Drago kicks, snaps, bites at Billy, taking small chunks from his forearm, dragging talons through the skin on the backs of his hands, but Billy drags him the length of the room.

"Billy! No! No Billy!"

Billy hears the cries of misery, the whistles, the jangling of the boots. The clomp, clomp, clomp of destruction.

Billy stares down at the face of his tormentor, his friend, his companion. His Master. Drago is the only kindness he has ever known, the only tenderness. Drago has given him his life. Every day he breathes is a day gifted him by his Master. These are the words he has heard upon every waking for as long as he can recall. Billy stares down at the face of the boy. Hardly a boy.

A hundred years old. A hundred years of death. It echoes again.

Drago spits and bares his fangs.

"I will tear your heart, beating from your chest! You will watch me swallow it whole! You filthy son of a…"

Drago screams as the light hits him, an unearthly shriek as his body begins to burn. His skin sizzles, crackles, and flakes away—consumed. Flames burst from his chest and his thin, white fingers smolder like kindling as they reach for Billy.

Billy squats next to him, and wonders at the lack of heat from the cinders that rise up and dance off in the breeze. Carrying away ten years of terror. A hundred years of death.

Billy stands, eyes watering in the blinding light of noon, turning at the sound of jangling metal at his back. More footsteps.

"He ain't one. He's not burning. Leave him be."

"Better get out of here, kid."

Billy squints into the dazzling light of a sun he has never known, makes out a shimmering figure ahead of him, long black coat, wide hat. The figure becomes two, two men stomping off to opposite sides of the dusty street. Billy rubs at his eyes with a bloody sleeve, then puts a hand to his brow to block the sun. He sees Rado's hat lying next to scattered piles of dust. He picks it up, dusts it off, sets it on his head. It is far too big, but cuts the sun enough that he can see.

Billy wanders away from the street, past more men in black coats, past more screams and whistles and jangling boots. Past the cattle, stumbling and confused, clambering over one another to nervously search their surroundings. These are not his people. Not since birth. He is different now. Alone. They are mere animals, waiting for slaughter. He comes to the gates at the edge of town. He doesn't look back. By sundown, Billy is high in the hills, looking down at the flames where his life had once been, watching the men as they mount their horses and ride away in the blessed light of darkness.

Billy sits next to a fire of his own making, a fire for himself alone. He is wrapped in the long black coat of the Prince of Night's Breed, clutching the strange spear that has set him free. The words are still playing in his ears. An echo that refuses to fade.

"You are the blood. That which flows from the Earth."

Billy looks out across the plains, beyond the smoldering ashes of his home.

"From the Night. To feed. To Fulfill. To bathe us in the blessed light of Darkness,"

Billy slides his arm free of the bulky canvas coat, eyes gleaming with tears as the flickering of the firelight plays against the white lines that run across his forearm.

"You are the blood, and the blood must flow."

Billy looks at his hands. The hands that have killed the Prince of Nights Breed. The Nights Breed that was now ashes and fire.

Billy feels the difference in his mind. He feels the freedom of his thoughts. He looks out across the vast ocean expanse of the black night sky.

He screams out. Again and again.

But there is nothing left for him there.

Billy holds the jagged shard of glass against his flesh, balancing it between the lines, the traces of Rado, the remnants of his existence.

"You are the blood," the words echo in his memory.

And the blood must flow.

DINNER IN CARCOSA

ALLAN WILLIAMS

The sky wept cold tears. The dreary landscape stretched out towards the horizon without a tree or piece of shrubbery to give it any color or hope. Tim couldn't fathom anyone living in such desolate country. The ancient road had long ago disappeared into the dusty earth and it was hard to imagine the cracked ground ever bringing forth any kind of life. Hours of travelling on horseback through the morose backcountry had begun to wear on his spirits. As the tempest threatened to grow in strength, there wasn't even the hint of browning fields or falling fences to break the monotony. Maybe it was a mistake to come this far alone?

From across the empty prairie, a frigid wind blew through the barn. Tim had been surprised to stumble across the sagging shelter just as the freezing rain started to fall.

"Better rain than hail, eh boy?" Tim said, stroking the neck of his horse. He walked it away from the open doors and further into the dry warmth at the back of the barn. The horse was a loan from the Wainwrights back in Iddersleigh. They had warned him against driving his car out here.

"Frankly, I don't know why you're headed out that way,"

Mr. Wainwright had frowned at dinner last night. "Carcosa's been abandoned for years, ever since the government moved all those families out during the Depression. The whole place just dried up and the wind blew the crops away. Nobody lives there now. It's a waste of time if you ask me."

Tim shrugged and accepted another helping of beets from Mrs. Wainwright. "My company says there's a policyholder out in Carcosa somewhere, so I need to go and pay them a visit, or at least take of photo of any hail damage I come across for our records."

Concern crossed Wainwright's face again and he glanced at his wife. Tim saw it and he attempted to change the subject, pointing his fork at his plate, "These beets are amazing, Mrs. W. I've never had anything like them. What is your secret?"

Mrs. Wainwright smiled, "Lavender. My grandmother used to say that lavender would keep away anything that might harm you. She put it in just about everything. Casseroles, cookies, tea, you name it. I'll give you some to take with you."

"Thank-you. This is simply delicious."

Tim had spent the night comfortably in the guest room despite the wind howling all around the homestead. The following morning Mr. Wainwright offered Tim the use of one of the family's horses, stating "Not a lot of gas where you're going. Not a lot of anything, really. Tallboy'll at least keep you company out on that lonely road."

Tim nodded. The old man was right. He had been gone from the city for a few days and the car was already pretty low on gas. He hadn't seen a lot of filling stations this far from Medicine Hat. The horse seemed like a good idea. Mrs. Wainwright had packed the saddlebags with food for him and Tallboy. Tim thanked the pair for the hospitality, promising to return sometime the next day.

Letting Tallboy set the pace, Tim waved good-bye to the family. As they made their way down the road to Carcosa, he pulled Mr. Wainwright's old weather-beaten plowing hat low over his eyes and thought about the last time he had been on horseback. Grade school and scouts, something his father had insisted Tim learn how to do. Like riding a bicycle or driving a car, his father had said. Tim was surprised how quickly it all came back.

The Wainwrights had been correct in their description of Carcosa as deserted. Only occasional patches of long grass broke the dry, cracked earth as Tim and Tallboy drifted along in the increasingly strong westerly breeze. Tim saw few signs of life and smiled with amusement, remembering how Mrs. Wainwright placed a branch of lavender in each saddlebag. "Horses smell bad enough," she said. "This might help you smell a little more pleasant if you do run into anyone out there."

He was about to check his map to see if he was in fact in Carcosa when he noticed that the sun had disappeared. Dark clouds covered the sky. Last week a hail storm had wiped out acres of crops through the region, and Tim began to worry about getting caught in another when the outline of the solitary barn graced the horizon. With the temperature falling and the wind gusting, Tallboy didn't need any encouragement to canter towards the open barn doors.

"That's the idea, boy. No sense in going to take pictures anytime soon," Tim said once they were under shelter. "More hail might come tonight or else this wind could knock something over and we'd have to go out all over again. Best hunker down and wait to see if the storm moves out in the morning." Hunker down was something his father always said whenever bad weather reared up while they visited his uncle's farm. Tallboy snorted in agreement and Tim took off the saddle, patting the horse down after the long trek, much like he remembered doing with his dad. He could almost hear his father's voice leading him through the steps.

"Let's see if Mrs. Wainwright packed you some treats in these bags," he said. He slipped the saddlebags off Tallboy and placed them on a nearby hook. He lifted the flap off one of the bags and a big whiff of lavender hit him hard in the nose. He took the small branch of lavender out and placed it in the other bag with his change of clothes before setting Tallboy up with the feedbag. As he did so, Tallboy started pawing at the ground nervously. Tommy looked up and thought he saw someone pass in front of the barn entrance. He looked around, half-expecting to see his father come around the corner, then tightened the bag around Tallboy and patted him on the neck. "Eat your oats and relax. You've earned a rest today. Bet that was just the wind."

A moment later however a voice called out in greeting from the front of the barn. Tim was shocked to see a woman in her early thirties, with long black hair and pale skin standing there, waving at him.

"Hello," he called back, "I didn't think anyone lived here anymore. Mind if we stay? We just didn't want to get caught in the storm. We'll be gone as soon as it breaks."

"No worry," the woman answered. She paused, putting a hand on her hip as if considering something, letting Tim get a long look at her. Her tongue darted across her lips as she smiled, "How about coming back to the house where it's warm? We'll be eating soon and you're welcome to join us."

Tim blinked. He didn't remember seeing any farmhouses. It was just the barn all alone, in the field, that had caught their attention from the road. Tallboy snorted and shook his head, forcing Tim to try and calm him again with another pat on the neck. "Sure. Will my horse be okay out here? I don't really see anything to tie him up with. I don't want him to wander off."

"We'll close the barn door," she said, waving Tim over. "My name's Sarah."

He shook her hand to introduce himself and was instantly warmed by her touch. As soon as he stepped out of the barn though, he saw the farmhouse looming large a few dozen feet away. It was impossible to think he hadn't seen it earlier. He looked at Sarah and then at the house. She smiled back at him again. I must have been tired from riding all day, he thought.

"You're lucky you came along when you did," Sarah said as they walked passed the empty hog pens and chicken yards that straddled between the barn and the house. Tim was shocked at how much he had missed. Off in the distance, lightning lit up the outline of a grain elevator. Sarah continued, "I think we're going to get a hard hit of rain any minute. It gets so loud and windy around these parts, during a storm you could have spent the whole night cold and alone in the barn and we might never have known you were out here."

"You guys get any damage from the hail?" he asked. Up close all the buildings seemed newer than he had initially supposed.

"Hail?" Sarah gave him an odd look. "No, it never hails around here."

They reached the farmhouse and Tim followed her inside, the storm door clattering behind them. She ushered him forward through a kind of boot room where empty shoe racks ran along the floor and coat pegs lined the wall. A lot of people lived here once, he thought. A strange bitter smell filled the house but it was warm; something Tim appreciated after all the chilly hours on the road. As they entered a long narrow hallway, Tim could hear noises coming from elsewhere in the building.

What looked like a tiny clapboard house from the outside was actually quite spacious. The hallway Sarah and Tim proceeded down was much longer than he had anticipated. Despite the poor lighting, the backlit frame of another door could be seen at the far opposite end. No windows or view holes anywhere broke the darkness of the corridor but, again, noises could be heard on other side of the walls. Sometimes, Tim even thought he could make out voices talking, though at other times it sounded more like growls or moans seeping out between the sideboards. Whenever he heard something, he'd shoot a glance at Sarah for an explanation or comment. But she moved ahead, undisturbed by the strange sounds. Eventually they reached the door.

She put her hand to the knob and found it locked. "Sherry," she called out as she knocked loudly. "I'm back, let me in."

Tim heard heavy weights tumble into place and the door slowly creaked open. Another young woman, slightly smaller than Sarah but with equally dark hair and pale skin, stood on the other side.

"This is my sister, Sherry," Sarah said as the two girls smiled at each other. Tim reached out to shake Sherry's hand. It felt surprisingly hard and dry, as if worn by years of working the land. The door opened into a kind of intersection; to their right was the now empty kitchen, and he followed Sherry and Sarah to the large dining room on the left where ten other people, all bearing a familial resemblance to the two girls, gathered around a table, ready to eat. Tim spied an empty space at one end of the table, where an odd-shaped crucifix hung on the wall. He looked to Sherry and Sarah to see if he should take the seat, but someone else rose and disappeared out another side door, quickly returning with an extra chair, putting it down by the corridor entrance side of the room.

Seated at the far corner next to the empty space was the oldest man Tim had ever seen. He spoke to Tim in a hoarse, but firm voice. "That's my father's chair. It sits open while we wait for his return."

Tim looked around the room. He couldn't imagine anyone even older hobbling in. "Where is he?"

"Somewhere up north," the old man replied. "It's been ages since we last heard from him."

Tim nodded, "A lot of families I've met around here have people working up north."

"He speaks to us of a black lake and black stars that bubble in the silver night," Sherry said. Her own coal black eyes unnerved him and the image of a black lake and black stars made him think of the vast northern tar pits rumored to stretch on forever.

"Sounds like it," he answered.

Beside him, Sarah smiled, as if sensing Tim's discomfort. "Pay no mind to Levi," she said, reaching over and putting her hand on his shoulder. "My uncle is just old and cranky. It's nice to have a visitor here for once." She looked around the table and saw everyone was seated. "Can we eat?"

There was a pause. Tim waited to see if anyone would say

Grace, and he found his gaze travelling down the table towards the strange crucifix that had caught his eye earlier. He was no longer sure it was a crucifix. Although the position of the central figure was the same, with feet together and arms outstretched, the clean-shaven man was not nailed to a cross. Instead, the cross form came from three pairs of angelic wings, one pointing below to his feet, another rising above his head, and the last outstretched behind arms.

"It belongs to my father," Levi said. Tim was caught off-guard by the curtness in the man's voice and could feel Levi's dark eyes on him. The solid black orbs created a darkness that threatened to swallow up the dim lighting in the room. Forcing himself to look away, Tim couldn't help but notice that all of the other dinner guests, or family members he suspected, had the same kind of eyes.

"Your father had interesting taste. It looks lovely." he offered in an attempt to appease the old man. A heaviness had descended upon the room with Levi's outburst and Tim watched the other man's face twist and tighten, like a piece of leather stretched over muscle. Levi frowned and down the line of the long table, Tim saw the same look reflected in all the faces. Only Sarah continued to smile.

Any further comment from Levi was cut short by the arrival of the salad plates, carried into the room by Sherry and another, much older woman. Sarah reached out and touched Tim's arm, whispering, "That's my aunt Bess, she doesn't hear so good."

He smiled at the old woman who handed him a plate filled with bitter smelling green and purple leaves. He recognized the smell as the same one he noticed entering the house. He waited for Bess and Sherry to finish serving all of the others before trying some of the purple leaves. Incredibly bitter, he did his best to hide his discomfort. Sarah watched him chew, grinning.

"It's an acquired taste, I know. Chicory," she explained. "Something of a family recipe."

Tim nodded and struggled to swallow, looking around for a glass of water or something to help ease his work. "There seems to be a lot of local specialties around these parts," he coughed, hoping someone would offer him something to drink. "I've tried a lot of secret recipes in the last few days."

Sarah raised an eyebrow and then watched Tim bravely venture a second bite, before motioning to her aunt for something to drink. Turning back to Tim, she asked. "What was it that brings you out to these parts? We don't often see travelling salesmen around here."

"I'm not a salesman," Tim tried to laugh, but it sounded like another cough. "I'm actually in insurance. I work for Gabrieli International. We're processing claims for all the people who suffered damage during the last hailstorm. I was on my way to Carcosa when the wind picked up and it looked like it was about to start raining."

Levi stiffened at the mention of Carcosa. "What do you know about Carcosa?"

"Nothing," Tim shrugged. "We have a policy on a homestead at Carcosa under the name Ambrosovich."

The sound of the name unleashed commotion all around the table. Bess dropped a stack of empty plates while Levi began banging the table loudly. Even several of the younger people exchanged shouts from across the room. "That's my father's name!" Levi bellowed. "How dare you speak it!"

Sarah raised her arms to quieten everyone. It took some time, but when there was a modicum of silence she spoke, her voice carrying an air of disbelief. "I'm sorry, there must be some mistake. That policy was registered with Hastur and Associates, some time ago. I believe you've come all this way for nothing."

Tim nodded, "Yes, it's pretty old for the region out here, but I assure you, it's one of ours. I've seen the file in our offices. Gabrieli International bought out Hastur and Associates a few years ago and acquired all their assets and policies."

This announcement caused even more of a ruckus, tinged with a degree of nervous energy. Tim wasn't sure what was going to happen next. Even Sarah struggled to maintain her composure. "I'm sorry to hear that. Hastur was a family friend. We don't get a lot of news from the outside world. Anyways, we didn't get any damage during that last storm, so again, I'm afraid you've come this way for nothing."

"Just being thorough," Tim shrugged. "Besides, if I hadn't come here, I never would have tasted this delicious salad Aunt Bess."

The old woman smiled and the family returned to their salads in silence. Tim slowly worked at his. As the others finished, Sarah looked down the table towards another middle-aged man, and then forced a grin at Tim. "You are very kind, but perhaps our next dish will be more to your liking. My cousin Aamon has prepared some truly outstanding steaks for us. Perhaps we might even beg of Levi for a few bottles of wine. He has some famed vintages hidden away in his cellar."

"Oh yes," Sherry clapped and left, as the old man frowned again. Bess rose to collect the plates. "Let's turn this into a real banquet, in honor of our guest."

Tim felt Sarah's hand on his thigh beneath the table and blushed, "Oh, I don't want to be any trouble."

"Nonsense." she smiled as tall, thin cousin Aamon rose and glared at him with those cold, black eyes, nostrils flaring as he turned and left the room. Tim was afraid to glance at Levi. He could feel the heat emanating from the other side of the table. Sherry and Bess returned quickly, the one carrying empty glasses for the wine, the other plates of savory steaks. After the dry, bitter leaves of chicory, Tim's mouth watered in anticipation. A few moments later, Aamon appeared with several bottles tucked under his arms.

"Enjoy," Sarah announced as the wine was poured.

No one spoke as they cut into their dishes. The meat was soft and tender, like something Tim expected to find at a fancy restaurant, a stark contrast to the salad. Succulent, it paired well with the heavy ruby red wine. He shook his head at the thought that he was eating this fantastic meal in a desolate farmstead in the middle of nowhere.

Tim had to rummage through the old map library for

several hours before finding any reference to the broken-down township. He checked himself. It had only appeared so during the storm when he was tired and couldn't see anything in the growing dark. The reality was that it was actually quite nice and comfortable here with the Ambrosoviches. He took another bite of steak and, as Sarah refilled his glass, he toasted the gathering.

"Delicious!" Tim said with a smile, made even larger by the cup of wine. "Sarah was right, Aamon, this food is outstanding! You could work in any of the finest kitchens back in the city."

Aamon grunted in return and sipped his wine. Tim took a few of his own and then looked around nervously. His glass was almost empty. He tapped Sarah on the arm and whispered, "Is there a washroom nearby?"

Sarah looked a little embarrassed, admitting "There's just the outhouse, by the barn, I'm afraid."

"That's alright," Tim replied. "I'll only be a few minutes. Please excuse me."

He rose from the table, slightly unsteady, and made his way to the door. The rest of the family kept eating although Tim thought he felt Levi's dark glare follow him down the long hallway. It was a much quieter walk this time. Probably nothing but the sounds of the family preparing the meal the first time around, he thought.

Outside, it took a few moments for his eyesight to adjust to the dark. He saw the outhouse, next to the barn as Sarah had told him it would be. Once more he was surprised he hadn't noticed it earlier. How tired had he been from riding Tallboy all day through the cold and wind? He caught a whiff of his own body as he relieved himself. Ugh. I smell bad, too. How can these people stand to sit next to me? Maybe I should get Mrs. Wainwright's lavender?

He moved from the outhouse to the barn. The barn door was still closed from when Sarah had slid it shut but it wasn't locked. Tim had to push hard to move it open again. With only the faint light from the house behind him, Tim couldn't see that far into the barn. Hands outstretched, he inched his way towards the back of the barn, looking for a post or railing to get his bearing. Eventually he stumbled onto the saddlebags and rummaged through them, the air instantly filling with the smell of the potent herb. Smiling, Tim placed the small stalks of lavender into his pockets and then realized something was wrong.

He had expected to hear the horse shuffling around in the back, or breathing in the cold, but inside the barn was quiet.

"Tallboy?" he whispered.

No answer came back from the dark.

Maybe Tallboy was sleeping, he thought, somewhere in the back. He took a few steps away from the post. The horse should be nearby. Nothing. He moved ahead again and then waited once more. Still nothing. The next few steps took him all the way to the back of the barn. His toe nudged something on the ground and he bent down to pick it up. It was the feedbag. With an air of panic, Tim searched around the empty barn. Tallboy was gone!

Where could he have gone?

"I knew I should have tied him up! How am I going to explain this to the Wainwrights?" he said out loud. Maybe Tallboy wandered off and would find his way home. It didn't really explain the closed barn door though. Could Aamon or someone have come out and closed it, after noticing it was open? Sarah did slide it closed fairly easily. Maybe it didn't latch properly. He turned back to the house, intent on asking Aamon about it even if the grim man set Tim's nerves on edge. All the Ambrosoviches did really.

Standing outside the barn, he noticed that the smell of the lavender was really strong. He took some of the stalks from his pocket and tossed them on the ground back towards the barn. Don't want to be too obvious, he thought. Looking back towards the farmhouse, he saw it again like he did before, shabby and rundown, tiny and with only a greasy window facing the barn that Tim didn't remember seeing on his first walk.

From the edge of the barn, he could see strange shapes

through the window, moving back and forth across the room. He inched forward hoping to get a better look, but didn't want to be seen by anyone inside. Each step towards the house and the window made his heart beat faster.

As the shapes became clearer, he couldn't believe what he was seeing. Boney limbs and appendages, dark tight skin stretched over hands and feet ending in claws and talons. Faces, grim and dusk with flat mouths opening and closing to reveal sharp, blood-drenched teeth. The shadows of man-sized creatures with six foul wings gathered around a long table.

Around the table, Tim saw hunks of bloody meat and bone, some pieces quivering and others still with clumps of hair and skin. Slowly, his mind put them all back together as the ground seemed to shift beneath his feet. He stumbled against the side of the house and looked back inside the window. It was Tallboy! The meaning of the empty seat, with its half-eaten serving of raw horse flesh at the side of the table, suddenly became clear.

Tim doubled over at the window and vomited. He heard a door open behind him and then clatter shut.

"Tim?" Sarah's voice called out in the darkness. "Are you okay?"

"No," he moaned. "Monsters are eating my horse. We have to get out of here." He turned to look at her, but it wasn't Sarah. It sounded like Sarah, but it wasn't Sarah. Where Sarah should have been stood one of the tall, bony creatures, reaching for him with its leathery claws.

"What's the matter Tim? You look ill," the thing with Sarah's voice said, then stopped. He watched it cock its nose-less head, as if sniffing at the air. It breathed in several times, nostrils flaring, then hissed, "Lavender."

The monster lunged at him, but somehow Tim twisted away and started running for the road. There was a whoosh of wind as the great wings unfolded and beat against the night air. It grabbed at him but Tim ducked and stumbled, scrambling for the shelter of the barn. The creature was above him, following angrily, and in a panic he grabbed at one of the saddlebags, swinging it defensively in the air. The creature hissed and retreated a few feet before swooping in again. Still on the ground, Tim swung again with the bag, connecting this time with the thing's bony arm. It was a feeble strike, but the monster screeched and flew back again. Scrambling to his feet, Tim wondered if there really was something in Mrs. Wainwright's belief in the protective power of lavender.

It was a brief thought, lost as his feet struggled to find a running rhythm on the rocky road. He heard more screams from somewhere behind him. Still wielding the lavender saddlebag in one hand, he risked a look over his shoulder back towards the farmhouse. More of the six-winged monsters had joined Sarah outside, but none of them made a move to follow him.

He kept on running.

COLD EGGS AND WHISKEY

R. OVERWATER

Percival slid a thumb between his collar and the bandage on his neck. Both were damp. He scowled. The stain forming there would be innocuous enough—but blood did not easily wash out of fine cotton.

He took a last look down at the bottom of the hill. Townsfolk were still picking through the wreckage of the toppled locomotives, and the afternoon breeze was light enough it didn't yet lift the scattered dust. The cool scent of yellowing tree bluffs carried through the blue sky. Two engines lay head to head, overturned rail cars trailing behind like the spines of ruptured snakes. One engine was scorched and sooty where the firebox had burst, fatally roasting the engineer who now lay on the bed next to Percival's.

A handful of men stood in conciliatory stances, heads tilted towards a large figure in a wide grey Stetson. They all glanced over at the growing pile of recovered luggage and Percival was heartened to see the protruding corner of his new steamer trunk. Within it would be the pipe, and wouldn't it be satisfactory to hold that right now?

Fortunately, there was only the presence of the doctor and

the engineer's corpse to endure, and the doctor's own opiates provided sufficient numbness. Percival turned back to the infirmary adjoining the Doctor's house. It was best he inquired about obtaining more soon—lest more visitors arrive, and the Fear along with them. That would be the undoing of everything.

"Mr. Hustinson. What do you make of the great spectacle we extricated you from?" The doctor was leaning across the engineer's bed, a wad of wet, ochre bandages in his hands. He looked up as Percival entered. "I trust the Sheriff is still down there, holding court?"

"It would appear so."

"A welcome turn I suppose. Often he is busy creating half the patients I treat."

"At this moment, he is preoccupied with the matter at hand."

The doctor dropped the bandages into a white enamel basin. "The whole event was excruciating to watch, I'll tell you. Tremendous luck for you all both trains were slowing to stop at the station."

Percival closed the door behind him. "I must say, this is quite the disaster."

"I suppose. Large disasters don't necessarily require great amounts of space. For me, there isn't anything more horrific than this. What fire does to the human body," said the doctor, nodding down to the oozing corpse as he rolled it up inside a sheet. "If you're here any length of time, someone will bring up the schoolhouse arson. I carried most of the children out, though you could scarcely tell that was what they once were. "

"The schoolhouse arson." It emerged from Percival's mouth more a statement than a question.

"Worst thing this town has ever seen. Had any of the children lived, they'd be about your age. Except for one who was truant that day, most locals here are either much older or younger than you as a result. "

Percival didn't answer. His tie felt unusually tight across his throat and he disrobed, climbing back into bed. Tomorrow he would embark into the countryside as planned. But not before he recovered his trunk. Without its contents, there could be another lapse. And here one couldn't hide in the faceless anonymity that a large city provided.

****

The dull light of the jailhouse was soothing. Thank merciful Christ. The sheriff had already gotten a bellyful of railway bureaucracy, missing baggage and cries for compensation from local merchants. More was sure to come. What a goddamned mess. But messes weren't the responsibility of the law. "So if you don't mind," he muttered to himself, "all of you who are able, collect your belongings and get the hell out of my town."

It would be days before the Houghton Number 3 could get through again, meaning a delay on dry goods from the east. The Mountaineer North would be even longer returning to service, but that was less of a concern. All it carried was Chinese, Mexicans and broke Alaska-bound prospectors who'd squeeze two bits so tight it made George Washington fart. Return trips usually carried hard-up and criminally desperate wretches, or whoring drunks so flush with gold their behavior was equally criminal.

Things seemed normal for the moment. Mostly because he was sitting inside rather than in his chair out front—his usual pleasure, not long available what with winter approaching. But in here, the whole catastrophe stayed largely out of mind. At least until he saw Artie Miller through the tiny square of the window, rolling up in his wagon.

Alongside Miller, the New York dandy he and the doctor carted up the hill two days ago sat primly, fiddling with his tie. The sheriff watched him tug it once more and step gingerly over the wagon side onto the worn plank boardwalk.

The hotel had not delivered breakfast yet when the sagging door pushed through its rut in the floor. There was the dandy, paused at the threshold. His glance across the room, from the figure splayed across the cell's cot to the sheriff's table and back to floor where he stood, was visibly deliberate. Timber dragged on timber, cutting the silence as he shoved the door shut again.

The dandy seemed slow to grasp that warm greetings weren't coming his way. What the hell did he want? The newcomer quietly cleared his throat. "Good morning Sheriff. My name is Percival Hustinson. The stationmaster says you are quite insistent that all passengers identify themselves to you before they claim their belongings."

Right. He had said that.

"I also wanted to deliver a proper thank-you for getting me prompt medical attention. From my perch up there, your efforts in this community were not unnoticed. I hope your town is as grateful as I am."

The sheriff grunted and reached across the table. "Bruce Sawyer." The dandy recoiled less than most as the sheriff's scarred mitt engulfed his hand. "I gather by this ride with Artie that you're done with our little town."

"To the contrary, Sheriff Sawyer. This is my journey's end. I've arranged through your good doctor to take room and board with a widow out of town. I'm told she is bereft of both income and the able labor required to maintain her property."

Sawyer mustered what cordiality he could. "Well, that would be Arla Rochette. Whatever you heard, she's not actually lacking for help. Or for company. I get out there myself to make sure things are looked after."

The door opened and the hotel kitchen boy bounced into the jailhouse, a wax paper bundle clutched against his stained apron. Sawyer ignored him. "Arla's got a son she needs to raise right, and you know women. They don't always know what's best for them. I've had to run off a few so-called suitors." His eyes focused on something outside the window. "She'll appreciate that someday."

The dandy brushed off his jacket. "Well. Mr. Sawyer, I am a man of respectable conduct, merely in need of suitable lodging."

"Fair enough. But you're clearly the refined sort. Some of the help she needs might be more back-work than you're used to."

"Perhaps at first. But you would be surprised, sheriff, what I am capable of once my blood is sufficiently up." He turned to the door and gestured towards the boy. "I will leave you to the more important matter of breakfast. Again, thank you for your assistance amidst all this calamity."

The sheriff stared at Percival's back. The rectangle of light in the doorframe narrowed, the room's shadows eclipsing the kitchen boy, leaving him and the sheriff divided by a sliver of light that thinned to nothingness. The latch clicked. In the time it took Sawyer's eyes to adjust to the previous gloom, it was surprisingly dark.

****

Arla Rochette gripped the edge of a wet sheet and snapped it away from her to eliminate any creases. She pinned it to the clothesline and moved quickly to the next item in the pile, making the most of the warm breeze that had sprung up. Its timing couldn't have been better, a nice addition to the day's good luck. Winter was coming, the pantry needing stocking, and there would be chores in knee-deep snow neither she nor the boy would be up to. This new boarder would be most welcome.

After Mr. Miller rode out with the news that a man was convalescing at the doctor's, and needed lodging in a day at most, her elation waned almost instantly. When she looked inside the guest room, shafts of sunlight illuminated blankets of dust, musty pillows and grimy walls. She'd sneezed immediately. Pulling off the goose-down quilts, she saw the sheets were more threadbare than she remembered. And all that linen had been so new and crisp on her wedding day.

Everything was new once, wasn't it? The town had rejoiced when a young blacksmith arrived and set up his much-needed forge, and it wasn't long after that he built a new homestead as solid as he was. A two-story house with a well shored-up root cellar, outbuildings and a barn; Arla was such a lucky young bride. She used to watch him through the kitchen window, cutting and fitting lumber sunup to sundown. Life blossomed around her, and withered just as quickly.

Today she was a mother on her own with a homestead just on the good side of beyond-repair. Boarders kept the pantry full—but they couldn't stop the gradual peeling of paint and the inevitable slump of rooftops. She and the boy were just the remainder of a stupid, short-lived man.

It didn't matter. If the new boarder stayed until spring, they would get by. A black dot appeared on the hilltop. She returned her attention to the laundry, pinning up the last sheet, and when she looked east again she could see that it was Mr. Miller.

Miller's passenger was half a head taller than him and dressed in a dark suit, a tie knotted tight against his collar despite the warm fall day. He sat straight as a gallows pole, in contrast to Miller who bobbed and swayed, absorbing the motions of the wagon as it rattled down the hillside.

They would need lunch. Hopefully Eli hadn't wandered halfway to the creek this time. There was water for the boy to pump; enough for a meal, the horses, and to draw a bath. The wagon turned up the dirt lane and the stranger's features were now visible. Such a handsome well-dressed man, wanting just-serviceable lodging outside a little town of no importance? Whatever the reasons, Arla counted her blessings. Taking the laundry basket under one arm, she went inside to put the kettle on.

****

There was something about the rays of the low-angled autumn sun that softened the landscape—as though one was peering through a thin layer of gauze. The dirty streets of New York were never graced by light like this. Percival dug one more hill of potatoes and stopped. Resting on his spade handle, he took a deep breath and savored the cool fall air.

There were distinct moments of contentment doing these chores—or what seemed like contentment—really, he had little to compare the feeling to. It was just yesterday he'd recognized this new arrangement as a chance to verse himself in rural practicalities. It would be necessary if he was to truly eschew the encumbrances he'd so recently fled.

"Please. From now on you must let me help you with these chores, Mrs. Rochette."

She'd looked up as she gathered the spilled armload of wood, wresting her grimace into a smile. "It's Arla. And it would surely be appreciated."

"Percival." Or, thinking far back, before he was thrust upon a train and landed at the doors of the orphanage—"Percy even. If you'd like."

Her smile broadened. "Percy. Have you ever split a whole cord of wood before?"

Winter came soon after, piling fat blankets of snow upon the land. The wind whipped them into thick drifts, fortifying Arla's property behind them.

"Maybe you can bring us wood and bedding straw next summer instead of the sheriff," the boy said through the barn door one afternoon. The light beaming through the doorframe was near-blinding. It framed the boy's silhouette and filtered through the cloud his breath formed in the cold air.

Percival grinned inwardly as he stabbed his pitchfork into a clump of straw, shaking it across the pen floor. "Sheriff Sawyer's attempts at woo are indisputably clumsy," he said under his breath. He spoke up. "Eli, his deliveries are a blessing you should not take for granted."

The boy stepped back, almost invisible in the light. "Mother says it would be better if it was you."

He watched the boy trod through the snow back to the house and shifted his gaze to the vista beyond. So much more peace than the library alcoves he'd hidden in throughout his youth. Even the merchants of the Orient and their smoky backrooms offered but an iota of what now surrounded him.

His decision had been the right one. Wherever he had this kind of space, he could live forever. And the fact that winter temperatures kept the number of callers down was a welcome revelation.

When he retired to his room that evening, he unwrapped the pipe, rolling its ivory stem between his fingers. He considered going downstairs and throwing it into the stove, its destruction a pledge to his new life. But spring would arrive soon enough, with uninvited visits by the sheriff and necessary trips to the town for supplies. Those were just the foreseeable hurdles. Any one of them could spell trouble. He took out his ink and paper and set about penning some long-delayed letters.

****

Arla was absorbed in Percy's words, her hands reflexively darning one of his socks, the timbre of his voice now a comforting regularity. She watched him curl his fingers into his palm, unconsciously fingering new calluses. The lamplight shimmered on the plaster walls. It was hard to say who anticipated these evening readings more; her or the boy, who always sat intently.

"O stay, three lives in one flea spare, where we almost, yea, more than married are," Percival continued, pausing to explain an occasional passage to Eli.

She didn't know the names of the books he read or their authors, or always understand what she heard. But his words were right and good, and so was everything else. After about a month or so, evenings began leading to pleasant wishes of goodnight, satisfying sleeps, and mornings with the kitchen already warm, the day's wood in the stove-side bin. The afternoons, when not forbiddingly cold, were spent walking by the frozen creek with Percy and Eli.

A week before, Percy had concluded a tale he'd been reading for several nights. In it, a young woman fell in love with a suitor from a family she was not allowed to associate with. In the end they both took their own lives, a demonstration of overwhelming love they could neither have nor overcome. She'd never heard a story like it.

Eli had already sleepily ascended the stairs. They habitually doused the lamps, turned down the damper and found themselves walking up together. As Arla turned to her room, she gently grasped his hand. He followed. She glanced back, seeing unmistakable reverence in his eyes, and something in her turned upon its side. She closed the door behind them and so began another new routine.

Now, the kitchen wasn't heated when she rose anymore. But the mornings, lying and talking, made rising to a cold house more than a fair trade. Percy told her of the orphanage in New York, his fear of crowds, and the sanctuary of a secluded library corner where books offered a boy both escape and education.

She told him of a young bride with early good fortune, sudden and unending sadness, and plenty about the local townsfolk and countryside. He was especially interested in the school fire. Understandable—it was an event still talked about, but the more she told him, the more he challenged the depth of her knowledge.

"This all happened before my family moved here, you know," she said. "I saw the door handles and the iron bar that was shoved through them. They're behind glass in the town hall. Everything else I know is second hand."

He rolled over and smiled. "Other than you, it's the only thing about this drab hamlet that's of any interest. A generation of children snuffed out. Barbaric. Cowardly perhaps."

She raised an eyebrow in mock distaste. "Perhaps? And it wasn't quite all the children. One was never accounted for. An odd, mousy boy they say. No one lived to say if he was in the room or not. Some of the children's bodies were... and the other, well you met him. He was late for school and got there when it was on fire. He got the bar out and one door open but it was too late."

"Well that explains his scarred hands. Your handsome suitor would be the last of his generation in this town, then. Possibly."

"Handsome... He's a lout. And being helpful fills the manger and tops up the woodpile. But that's all."

She turned over and reached for the bedclothes, feeling a kiss land below her shoulder. Her skin tightened from the cold air that slipped beneath the covers as she brought her armload back. "Percy?"

"Yes."

"We don't have to be so careful. I'm not worried about an

unmarried woman's honor. And the worst that could happen is Eli will have a brother or a sister when I'm gone." She looked at Percival.

His look was almost one of pity. "There are always worse things than what one can imagine."

She must have looked puzzled, because his expression relaxed instantly. "You lovely, lovely thing. There is so much uncertainty in our lives and this is all so new. Please hear me when I say our precautions are of utmost importance. Introducing a fourth mouth to feed at this time would be disastrous. It is important that it's just the three of us for now."

He smiled. "I promise you. I live for the day when there are no fears whatsoever, and I can indulge your every wish."

****

A last-gasp snowfall had prolonged the mud outside and Sawyer could hardly tell where the street ended and his dirty floor began. Not that he was the only one sweeping out a busy room in a busy town. Prospectors were breaking camp now that it was warm enough to push north, the Houghton was running full and farmers were stocking up as they readied for spring seeding.

It would be nice to put the chair back outside once things dried up. But right now his hands were full with train passengers in the restaurant and a bar full of southbound sots with too much new wealth for their own good. Them and the gamblers and troublemakers they attracted. So the Chinaman that walked into the room didn't seem out of place at first.

His long single braid was thick, pushing at the back of his silk cap, and his knee-length tunic shone with elaborate embroidery. Sawyer had been sheriff at a railway junction long enough to have seen his sort.

The nature of the visitor's inquiry was unique though. Sawyer hadn't forgotten about the New Yorker out there with Arla all these months. It was a full day's ride in the winter, one-way, when the snow was as deep as it had been this year. That prevented him from checking on her and a winter's worth of thinking was coiled inside him.

"He's not, as you say, living there. He's just lodging for the winter. And I have to ask why you've come all this way to find him."

The Chinaman blinked and paused. The bastard was trying to think ahead of him and that always meant trouble. "There is a message I must bring," the man said. "I will find my way. Thank you, Sheriff." He did that odd little Oriental nod and turned for the door.

Annoyance ate at Sawyer well into the afternoon. He didn't like it when someone else shut a conversation down. Time for a visit to Arla's place.

Riding to the property next morning, he could see a hell of a lot of crows circling in the distance. He pushed his heels into the belly of his horse and cantered into the yard. Someone darted between the woodshed and the barn. He yanked the reins left but then caught sight of the house's open kitchen door on the right. Tugging back to stop, he swung off the horse. Resisting the urge to grab his rifle—he didn't want to scare Arla—he strode purposefully to the door.

The kitchen table was upended and chairs were strewn everywhere. The stove was overturned and a large cast iron fry pan lay on floor beside it. Blood was pooled around it. Sawyer studied the scene for only a second before running out the door.

He found the dandy in back of the barn, wild-eyed and frantically trying to bridle the aging draft horse. A leg, shoe sole to the sky, extended from behind the un-split cordwood over by the woodshed. A matching shoe, still laced, sat a few feet away.

The first blow caught the dandy squarely under his jaw, crumpling him and seating him awkwardly in the grass. With all his weight, the sheriff put his boot heel up into the disheveled New Yorker's nose, feeling it crunch from the force of the kick. And that was that. He hogtied the unconscious prissy with the bridle; one rein for his ankles, the other for the wrists, enough length left over to bind all four limbs together behind his back. More restraint than needed, but he enjoyed doing it.

Sawyer walked to the woodpile and slipped a toe beneath the body, rolling it onto its back. Whatever happened, the Chinaman must have seen it coming. Briefly anyways. The back of his head was untouched but his forehead was stove in. His jaw was broken, hanging slackly, and his features were obliterated, the nose little more than a smear. What the hell. The man would have been dead long before the bludgeoning stopped. Hard to believe this came from the wisp of a man trussed up in the grass over there.

The rattle of a wagon axle snapped Sawyer out of his thoughts. He pressed up tight to the woodshed and peered around the corner, not believing his eyes. It was Arla. Her hair was loose, blown back by the breeze as she rode up, dress exposing her bare shoulders. Her skin shone with a burnished glow that could only come from wind and sun.

The boy had already run in and now emerged with two gunny sacks, hoisting them over his head into the back of the wagon. It was brand new. The draft horse was also new, a bay Clydesdale. Property aside, Arla was poor. Everyone knew it. He looked more closely. Crates and sacks filled most of the back. *She was going with him.*

Sawyer looked over at the porch rail he rebuilt last summer. The new outhouse he'd built three years ago. She was going to leave with *him*. The boy spotted Sawyer and lowered his head—he'd learned well what the sheriff always meant when he pointed to the barn. *Go. Stay there and don't come out until I'm gone.* Sawyer took a deep breath and stepped up into the kitchen.

Arla had her back to him, frantically stuffing pantry items into a gunnysack. Sawyer measured his words. "I can't let you make this mistake. It's for your own good."

She whirled around, her expression pure fire. "You've always known what's best for me, haven't you? This whole county knows it and is too scared to say otherwise." Her chest heaved and she wiped a bead of sweat from her forehead. A glint beneath the ice box caught Sawyer's eye, and he stooped to retrieve a tiny two-round pistol, still cocked. He thumbed the hammer back up and jammed it into his pocket.

"What kind of good boy has an accomplice to murder for a mother? What's a boy like that turn out to be?" Her eyes didn't change, but her shoulders dropped slightly. He stepped forward and grabbed her left arm. "Look. By now you must know that me and you—"

Her hand flew out of nowhere and he just turned his head out of the knife's path, feeling a shallow sting across his cheek. His fist exploded into her mouth and she crashed into a shelf of pans, falling among them as they clattered. She glared up at him, cheeks flushed, pushing her hair from her eyes and wiping blood from her lip. If she wasn't already his, she soon never would be. Before he knew what he was thinking he was upon her.

She didn't cry out, resist, squirm, anything. It was over quickly. What he had just done was dawning even as he pulled her dress back down. She refused his outstretched hand. A fly buzzed and bumped against the kitchen window.

Sawyer motioned towards the barn. "He's a murderer now. I have to take him to jail, then I'll come back. I'll make this right Arla. Let me prove it. It'll take a while but we'll be all right when this is over." She shot him a look of sheer hatred. She would need to cool down before there could be any reasoning with her.

The trip back was silent, not even a whimper from behind on the saddleback. As he trotted up to the jail, Sawyer considered getting the doctor to set the dandy's nose but easily talked himself out of it.

When he finished shoving Seth Oettker down to one end of the cell's lone bunk against his oily, snoring brother, he rolled their equally drunk buddy onto the floor, propping him against the wall. He cut the dandy's bindings, making a mental note to visit the tack store and replace them, and tossed the dandy onto the bunk with the Oettker boys. He sure was a sorry sight for a killer; nose still bleeding, squinting through swollen eyes.

Sawyer locked the door and dabbed at the wound on his

own face. It was probably a good idea to run up the hill and have the doctor take a look before checking on Arla. "Rest up, you son of a bitch. You've got a whole shit-pile to answer for."

****

What Percival wouldn't have given for the pipe. As the aches from the sheriff's blows set in deeper with each step of the horse, the Fear that seized him in Arla's kitchen subsided. But now it was back. His eyes were still not adjusted to the dim light when he was unceremoniously deposited onto the fetid mattress, so he hadn't the chance to do a proper head count. He hardly needed to.

The ringing in his ears kept escalating and the air was hot and thin. One, two, three; there were four of them in this tight space and his heart hammered behind his rib cage. His eyes swam and he forced them shut, pressing his belly into the mattress and clenching the slender bunk rail. He knew what he had to do, but took a minute to wallow in denial like always. They were asleep. If he acted right now—someone mumbled and an invisible weight crushed Percival's skull from all sides.

He fought to collect fragments of more important thought: the implications of a visit from Fong's debt collector, the fate of Arla and her dear, sweet son if he failed to extricate himself from this.

But the pain was too pure, white, blinding. He let Fear-driven purpose push through it and tore a long, slim strip from the sheet balled up against the bunk wall. He rolled off the bunk and crept towards the mumbler on the floor, leaving the deepest sleepers, as always, for last. Rising to his feet and gently pulling the man's head and torso away from the cell bars, he slipped down behind and straddled him, wrapping his legs above the man's waist as he whipped the cloth strip around his neck.

Jerking it as tight as possible he spun the two ends around each other, twisting them into a rigid noose, taking care to leave no slack. Gripping tightly with his legs, he jammed his elbows over the man's shoulders and braced himself.

The man stiffened, then gurgled and bucked, trying to rise

to his feet. Percival kept his legs wrapped tight, leaning back to provide as much dead weight as possible. The man fell over, slapping and clawing behind his head. Burying his face in the man's neck to protect it, Percival rode out the bucking until it stopped. The man shuddered a few times, Percival still clinging to his back. Percival waited until he had been still for a few minutes and felt around his neck, removing the chain he'd detected.

The chain had a key on it. He stood, stepped across to the bunk and thrust it, two quick jabs, into the eyes of one man, then screwed it into the sockets of the other before the first victim's howls rose in earnest. Leaping onto the bed, he stomped his heel into the first man's nose, stomping and stomping, mashing it to a pulp while dancing around the vain fumbling of the other one.

When the target of his kicks fell still, he strangled the other blinded man with his bare hands, weathering a few random blows to his swollen face. As that man fell lifeless, Percival returned his attention to the bloody, unconscious mess alongside him and made sure the job was finished.

Eyes did not bleed much, he noted. He, on the other hand, was gushing profusely through his nose and he tried wiping it with his sleeve. But the sheriff had rendered it too sore to touch. He removed his soiled shirt, dressed the man on the bed in it, and composed him, face to the wall, in as realistic a sleeping pose as he could. Spreading the mumbler out in front of the cell door so there would be no mistaking a dead man, he lay face down beside him with the bed sheet pulled over his head and upper body.

It was a terrible shame. Only one of them needed to die to restore the balance. But there was never any stopping. What was important was that he had defeated the Fear once more, and his thoughts were again his own. His ears no longer roared, his heart ceased pounding and the ache in his nose throbbed to the front of his attention. He waited to hear the sheriff's footsteps. Any hope of seeing Arla again would hinge on the first few seconds after he did.

****

Something—a coyote, Sawyer guessed—had started in on the Chinaman's body. Crows and magpies were doing their best to consume the rest and Sawyer shooed them away, unfurling the swath of brown canvas he'd brought with him. The body securely bundled, he went into Arla's house. He corrected himself: into the murder scene.

Arla hadn't wasted a minute after he'd left. The pantry was cleaned out and the wide-open, empty cupboards were plain to see from the kitchen door. Her largest cast iron skillet was still on the floor. Closer inspection revealed thick smears of blood, and dried bits of more-than-just-blood. Sawyer shook his head. How you could enter a house armed and lose the upper hand to that pasty girl of a man was beyond him. He set the pan down and climbed the stairs, liking what he found there even less.

The dandy's trunk was in Arla's room, not the guest room where it should have been. A few items still littered the bottom. The pillows on each side of the bed bore recent impressions and the bedding was folded back on both sides. Sawyer clenched his teeth and pawed through the remaining items in the trunk.

He opened a small hardwood box, recognizing the contents for what they were immediately. The intricately carved pipe spoke of greasy yellow men in filthy dens where good folk never went. Beneath the pipe was a leather folio around a sheaf of papers.

At the top of the pile were two recently sealed envelopes addressed to two different doctors in Austria, of all places. Below that was a letter to the dandy, from a Mr. Hall at Clark University—an uppity eastern institution, Sawyer guessed—referring to some sort of illness the dandy had.

"My attempts to entice the world's two leading thinkers on the human mind to come and speak in America have been resisted so far," the letter said. "As such we cannot yet draw upon their research to determine why this specific number of people triggers your episodes. Bringing all the education and experience I myself can bear upon your problem, I cannot settle upon an answer."

Men of letters did not often trade words with Sawyer, and the reading was slow going. He persevered.

"Moreover, I must admit to being significantly troubled by the undertones of your correspondence. If your episodes are truly as you describe them, I envision both the room's occupants and yourself as being in great jeopardy. I find, in your letters, inferences that you have succumbed more than once and it is difficult to believe that someone has not been grievously injured. While I endeavor to find you help, I implore you to seek the solace of sparsely populated places and, if warranted, speak to the proper authorities about any deeds that may be weighing upon your conscience."

Below that was a tattered New York Times clipping about an orphanage fire that killed dozens. Sawyer felt a knot forming in his gut. An old photograph was beneath the clipping; a woman. Did she not resemble the spinster who once lived a mile east of the schoolhouse with her bastard son? The remaining piece was an aged envelope addressed to New York. Sawyer opened it and almost fell over.

He held a well-creased page from the Oracle, the town's original newspaper. The story on it was about the schoolhouse arson. He didn't need to read it. Leaping to his feet, he sprinted down the stairs, two at a time.

****

Flames were crawling up the west side of the jailhouse as Arla rounded the street corner. She pulled up to the jail and swung her legs over the rail, sliding down to the street and running up to the doorway. "Get under that tarpaulin and don't you dare peek out!" she yelled to Eli.

There was no telling what happened while she was stocking up at the flourmill. All she knew was that somehow, she had to get Percival out of a barred cell and she was petrified. Not even a fry pan as a weapon this time, and away from the home she'd at least felt compelled to defend. Sticking her head through the open doorway, she tasted the bitter smoke. Her eyes watered but she could make out the sheriff, limping across the room, revolver in hand, something jutting from his thigh. It was a fountain pen.

Arla stepped across a body, then another; Sawyer's poker cronies, often deputized when the trains brought too many drunks through. The last one lay face up, a bullet hole in his cheek, head surrounded by a thick, dark puddle. The dry click of an empty gun cut through the flames' roar and she saw Percival, cornered between a safe and a tall cabinet, one of the sheriff's pistols in his wavering hand. He was shirtless, ribs smeared with blood, eyes like glazed porcelain. They widened as he identified Arla through the thick gouts of smoke.

Percival dropped the pistol. The sheriff holstered his own, oblivious to Arla's presence. "I know who you are, *Poor Percy*," he bellowed, snatching a pair of leg irons from the timber pole at the room's center. "You never should have come back."

"And you," grunted Percival, hooking his fingers behind the cabinet, "shouldn't have been tardy." He heaved the oaken weight of the cabinet forward onto the sheriff, dislodging a single cuss word as it flattened him. Arla leapt at Percival, smothering his mouth with her own, and seized his arm. He faltered as she dragged him out to the wagon.

She squatted beneath him and shouldered his weight with all the strength she could find. Heaving him up onto the bench seat, she followed and snatched up the reins, urgently smacking their length against the horse's rump.

****

Sawyer had gone to bed drunk without stoking the stove or filling the woodbin again, and thick frost lined the windows. He hobbled through the kitchen, pulled a coat off its hook, and went out to the woodpile. His leg hurt like a sonofabitch. It hurt when it was cold, and it hurt when it was going to get cold.

Summer hadn't been worth a tinker's dam, neither had the fall and winter was worse. The poorly repaired jailhouse was cold and drafty now and his injuries protested regularly. The whole town watched him stumble under his share of the pallbearers' weight and no one sure as hell wanted the deputies' jobs now—so help was scarce. And then there were the Oettker boys. They'd always been a handful, but no one had issues enough with them to forgive their death under the sheriff's care.

Too many dead people. And on top of all that, the railway company had decided that not only were improvements to the station and switching yard in order, it made sense to add another eastern line while they were at it. These parts of the west, they said, were a growth destination. Godammit all. He scooped up some wood and limped back into the house.

When the stove was good and hot he threw a pan on and heated a knifeful of lard till it sizzled. He scrambled up a half dozen eggs and took yesterday's mail down from the shelf. A thick envelope from the Alaskan Marshal who'd arrested the dandy was in it. Sawyer was surprised at the speed of the Marshal's reply but then, there had been a lot of surprises lately. He set the pan of eggs on the table and pulled up a chair, stuffing a forkful in his mouth and unfolding the newspaper page enclosed with the Marshal's letter.

They'd hung the dandy only a few days after they found the murder scene. The news page had plenty of details on the hanging, the accused's eagerness to see the gallows and the elaborate last meal prepared by the judge's own cook—a concession to the extraordinarily cooperative behavior of the murderer. Hustinson had spilled an unprompted flood of confessions; the school fire, countless deaths in New York, a jailhouse down south, and of course the crime that brought on the trial—the cabin bloodbath with the woman, the boy and the infant.

Sawyer read the article twice.

He only got a few lines into the accompanying letter before reaching for the whiskey, unreturned to its proper place in the cupboard for weeks now. The article was difficult enough to take. But the Marshal's detailed account of the crime scene, Arla dead, no one to protect her, dead children in her arms— he was obviously unaware Sawyer personally knew the victims.

"It was," the Marshal had penned, "as if someone had thrown a pail of blood into the cabin."

The whiskey cup was empty. Breakfast was barely touched. He'd probably been staring at the letter, more so than reading it, for nearly an hour, he figured. He pushed out from the table, eased himself up and stepped outside to the barn. The softened scent of manure, dried, aged, crumbling to near-dirt, was somehow comforting.

He pieced through the disarray, brushing down the dust and bits of bedding straw. There was an old milk stool among discarded tack and broken pitchfork handles. Surveying his surroundings, he realized the building was in better shape than the peeling paint and neglected interior indicated. The rafter above him was as straight as ever, an empty pulley for the loft's bale hoist awaiting the new rope sitting in the corner along with other abandoned hardware.

Looking down, he scuffed the straw and manure back with his boot, exposing a rough circle of floorboard. The planks were still solid; no rot and only a couple of nail heads working their way up. "Still a few more good years in this old barn," Sawyer figured. But not for him.

He straightened a few things along the wall, setting the milk stool over by the rope and other tools. His mind was still on the Marshal's letter as he walked back to the house.

Beautiful Arla Rochette. Dead. The boy and a new baby, murdered before they were even as old as Sawyer's schoolmates. The oddly coincident timing of the birth. The dandy killing a woman he'd moved heaven and earth to be with. All that, along with what he thought he knew about the killer's mental condition. No matter how he lined the facts up, they led him to the same place.

Sawyer may not have been overly schooled, but he could subtract nine months from a calendar date. So sure, the dandy deserved to hang a dozen times over for the schoolhouse, the Oettker boys, the Chinaman and God knew what else. But in that Alaskan cabin, he was just an accomplice.

The culprit who actually set the deed in motion wasn't there when it happened—but was responsible nonetheless. That man deserved to hang on suspicion alone. And hang he would.

But unlike Percival Hustinson, there would be no fine meal prepared for him. Just cold eggs and whiskey.

DEATH IS DAILY

CRAIG GARRETT

Tall resisted the urge to tell the Woman he was a product of rape.

He smiled as an act of submission, only to reveal the rows of thick edged teeth set in his jaw like some sort of demonic bear trap. She let out a noise that reminded Tall of a yipping dog.

"The Boy tells me there is work on your land."

The Woman was surprised by his voice, a deep whisper.

"Farm work," she said.

"I would enjoy to do farm work for you."

She glanced down at her boy, standing to the side and just behind Tall. He shook his head yes, beaming in a way she had not seen since he was an infant.

"Where you from?" she asked.

"Walcott Shire."

"You come that far east on foot with no weapons?"

"Yes ma'am."

She thought of the forest between her land and Walcott. The things like him that lived inside of it.

"You speak my language good."

"He was raised by our kind," The Boy said, no longer able to hold in his excitement. The Woman narrowed her eyes to shush him, and glanced back at Tall.

"You believe in the One God?"

"Yes, ma'am."

She looked him over again. He carried nothing save a small canvas bag and the ragged clothes on his back. She huffed, then went inside the house, which was made of mismatched field stone piled up and chinked with daub. Tall thought it looked sturdy for an isolated home some distance from a village.

The Boy yanked on Tall's three fingered hand, bigger than a boar's head.

"I told you she would let you stay. See?"

Tall figured it was more likely that the woman was grabbing a weapon, and anticipated her coming around the corner with a pitch fork or, worse, screaming for the monster to get off her land. He wondered if it would be possible to retain his anger. To not devolve as his guardians had insisted he would with age. To not take the woman. To not rip open their pink flesh and devour them.

She came back with a blanket.

"You sleep in the donkey stable," she said, tossing the blanket at Tall.

"The donkey is dead," the Boy whispered.

"You be up before me working. I'm not going to teach you how to farm what little we got. You know it already or best be moving on."

"I like farm work," Tall grinned, doing his best to conceal his teeth.

****

Tall was younger than the Boy when he learned that he had no soul.

His guardians made him read from the One Book every night, and prided themselves on teaching an unclean being such as himself not only to be literate, but to have faith in the One God. They came upon a passage. It spoke of how the

One God made man alone in his image, and that ogre folk were made by the Beast of the Sea. That man had come from the sky above, and upon death would be allowed to return to the light, while the ogre folk would be plunged back into the darkness of the sea, into nothingness. Tall wondered aloud which way his spirit would be permitted to go. His guardians guffawed, amazed he would ever think himself up for consideration.

"Tall, you are of your father's seed. He was a giant, like you. Be thankful you are permitted to live at all, and know you are blessed to live among the righteous, though you are wicked. Think not of a heavenly reward, for you will not gain one. Only the Depths await you."

And Tall was thankful.

****

She permitted him to eat supper with them that first night. She asked for Tall to sit on the floor, but still at the table. This was partially out of respect for her husband, but also out of fear that the Thing would break her stool under its great weight. They sat, the Boy next to Tall, and the Woman across from them both. She glanced at Tall, who took up nearly his entire side of the table, the Boy hanging on a corner, struggling to sit as close as possible to the Thing.

"Would you lead us in prayer?"

"Yes Ma'am," Tall said. He gave a simple and humble prayer the Woman approved of.

The meal was a soup, sopped up with rye bread. Along with water, they drank goat milk, which Tall had never had before but enjoyed.

"We met yonder on the creek bed," the Boy said. "He was drinking from the creek, on all fours, like a big pup."

The Woman watched as her son's feet bounced in place, as his hands shook with excitement. "On all fours?"

"I was thirsty. I did not... I did not stop to take the time to cup the water with my hands."

"Biggest tongue I ever saw!"

The Thing smiled at the Boy for the first time in the

97

Woman's presence. This too she approved of, despite herself.

****

They feared Tall. The ones that raised him pretended not to, but he grew to understand that they did and were perhaps even more afraid than the others. He heard his guardians tell curious visitors and strangers that Tall came to be when the ogre folk pillaged Walcott Shire years ago and raped his mother. She died giving birth. Tall, even as a newt, ripping her beyond repair. Her husband left Walcott Shire, joining the other men in fighting back the ogre folk, but he never returned.

Tall's guardians were elderly even when he was a child, but they were followers of the One God, and knew that fostering their beliefs into the deformed infant could make him an example to others.

Tall was only permitted to do hard labor. Many days his guardians loaned him out to haul wood. Eventually he was expected to uproot trees in their entirety and he did so without complaint. He would gather fieldstone to make houses and often, alone, he would reap and bind harvests in a day. A feat that would normally take a lone man a week to complete.

The village grew to appreciate Tall, but as prized livestock, not as a person. He was not permitted to look them in the eyes or speak in their presence.

But he smelled the fear in their sweat, and heard the dread in their high pitched, stunted speech. Their pale flesh was prone to injury, compared to his own robust gray skin. Their teeth were dull, small and useless in contrast to his sharp, multiple-rowed fangs. Everything about them delicate and weak.

He did not yearn to be one of them.

****

The Woman had a surprising amount of land.

Tall thought nothing of allowing the Boy to secure a plow intended for oxen to his waist, and did not protest when the boy playfully barked orders at him as to what areas of the ground needed breaking. The Woman offered the Boy and Tall breakfast, which he declined as he saw it as gluttony to dine so early in the day. However, Tall ate heartily at dinner and found himself looking forward to supper as the Woman prepared it.

During the day's work the Boy flattened the earth Tall had pulled up, and Tall found him to be a good worker for his age and size.

"How high do you figure you stand?"

"Nearly nine feet. I was told my kind never truly stop growing. Reckon I could grow more, but it slowed some three summers ago."

"Maybe you could loan me out some of that growing, Tall. I don't figure I've grown in three summers neither."

"You will. You're not much more than a baby."

"Shit, I ain't no baby."

He grinned, amused both by the Boy's cursing and the fact that he did not stand above Tall's waist.

"You already done more work before afternoon than our old workers did in a whole day. And there was seven of them."

"Where are they?" Tall asked.

"Dead. This past fall, bandits come out from the west. Killed em. Messed up our crops. Even killed the donkey. Momma says it run off in the commotion but I figure they killed it. They would've killed us too, but Momma hid us away over in tall grass. They burned down our real house. The one we stay in now is what was left of one the workers' homes."

"Your Father?"

"Dead. How come you're not a fighter, Tall? The Kingdom recruits in Walcott, yeah?"

"I served for some time, but was only allowed to do labor."

"How come you never got to fight?"

"They feared arming me."

"Well dadgum that's stupid. You're bigger than any ogre folk I ever seen."

"Where have you seen ogres?"

"In town a couple of times. Seen one dead on display at the gates. Saw another one hung for raping a lady. You way bigger than both of them for sure."

Tall's guardians had told him that he would grow larger than standard ogre folk due to his mixed blood. He did not tell the boy this.

The Boy dropped his rake and stepped onto the plow. Tall paid no mind as the child climbed from the plow onto his back. He continued to break the earth as the Boy prattled on into his ears. Tall wondered how long this child would be warm towards him.

But for now Tall was well fed and clothed and wanted for nothing.

He mostly dug graves for the men killed in combat. They would be buried not far from where they were killed. Only those with ties to nobility would be transported back to their homes for a formal burial. The slain ogre folk would be burned in a mass pile. The regiment's cleric would speak over the dead humans, to call upon the One God. He would say that the One God had made death daily and so it was good. Tall envied the men being allowed to join the light that would be denied to him.

He thought of the Depths and hung his head in dread.

****

The Boy insisted.

"Let's go in here and get ourselves a drink!"

Tall glanced at the tavern and back to the Boy. In Walcott he had been permitted to drink at taverns when escorted by his guardians. They were long dead.

"Ain't nobody going to mess with you. You're with me!"

The Boy yanked Tall's hand and led him inside.

It was early enough to be populated only by the elderly and Tall was relieved. The Boy went straight up to the counter. The barkeep was bemused.

"I ain't serving that thing nuthin' that'll get it drunk."

"Shit, Tall's too big to get drunk. No reason for the shakes, we just want cider."

The barkeep poured their drinks and the Boy paid him. The old men stared at Tall and the Boy as they sat at a table and had their drinks.

"Good, yeah?"

"Yes, thank you for buying it."

"No worries. Momma gave us plenty of coin to get more seeds and such. You a good worker and you're gonna get us back and running again. We'll get back to it here shortly."

A pair of men entered. One was layered with muscle and had a broad sword slung on his back. The other was older, but seemed gnarled and somehow toughened by age. He had a short sword drawn at his side. They both had ogre scalps adorning their shoulders.

They balked at the sight of Tall.

"Now, Douglas you best keep to yourself," the barkeep stammered in place. "The kid brought it in, and he's a regular."

The two men took seats at the bar and both turned to face Tall and the boy as they sat. The barkeep set two beers on the counter for the men. They did not pay.

"You best enjoy your fruit drink there, big fella. Gonna be your last." the older one said.

"Shit, we might buy a couple more rounds." the Boy said.

The men traded sideways glances and chuckled. The big one took a swig of his drink, spit it in Tall's direction. The liquid spattered at Tall's feet.

The Boy stood up, marched over to the muscled man, grabbed his beer and dumped it in his lap.

"You little shit!"

"Well damn, I ain't the crack shot with my lips that you are buddy. I got to improvise."

The older man stood up, sneering. "My tolerance done run thin, boy. You fetch your Daddy so I can have a word."

"He's dead."

"Explains a lot, boy. Your momma shacking up with that ugly buck over there?"

"Better him than you."

"We done talking." The older man nodded at the muscled one and he stood and drew his sword.

Tall finally stood. He stepped towards the door, his eyes averted to the floor.

Douglas the barkeep perked up. "He's going fellas. Why don't you all let me get you another drink? I even have some grapes that you all can have."

They paid Douglas no mind and stepped ahead of Tall.

The Boy wedged between the two sides.

"Put your weapons down. I don't want Tall to hurt you too much. I got me a heavy conscience. I couldn't live with myself if he hobbled your sorry asses."

The older man smacked the Boy across his face and pulled at the child's hair.

"You're lucky no one pays good coin for the scalps of little shits," he said.

The Boy struggled but couldn't get out of his grip. The older man stared at Tall.

"I tell you what," he said. "You, me and my buddy here can go outside the gates. We'll do you good with mercy, real quick. The boy don't have to see his prize pet get himself killed. What do you say?"

Tall looked at the Boy.

The muscled one smirked.

"Thing don't talk," he said.

The older man jerked the Boy back and he let go a whimper.

"Figure this little shit does enough talking for the both of them anyhow. Figure it might do him some good to see big bear here sent back to the Depths where he belongs. Figure he's gonna…"

Tall was upon him, gripping the arm the older man held the Boy with and twisting it until it snapped it clear, the arm going floppy as though it contained no bone.

The muscled one gasped and swung his sword, but Tall uprooted a bar stool and parried the attack, shards of wood scattering the room. Tall backhanded the man, sending him over the counter and crashing into bottles along the wall.

The older man sat on the floor, holding his useless arm and bellowing gibberish.

Douglas produced a loaded crossbow from behind the

counter and fired it. The bolt sailed past the Boy's face and hit Tall in the thigh, sticking in several inches.

"Well shit, Douglas! We're paying customers!" the Boy cried out.

****

Tall was confident that the humans would not follow him and the boy far into the forest. Truth be told, Tall had only been through the forest once alone, and had been fearful the entire time. He decided to follow the nearest north path, where he had been told wild beasts roamed, but were too fearful to attack a thing of his size.

The Boy did not have the sense to be afraid.

"I swear, Tall! You jacked their jaws good!"

Tall did not answer as he sprinted through the woods, the Boy sitting on his shoulders, holding the mane of his hair as reins.

"Aw, you don't pay this any mind. You didn't kill nobody! Shit, I say we go back to my Momma's house."

"I will not jeopardize her along with you. I will return you to your mother soon and be on my way."

The Boy lost his breath.

"Tall, c'mon now. It ain't right for you to talk that way."

"It is right, boy. I endanger you as long as I stay."

The Boy yanked at Tall's mane.

"Stop your running!" he shouted.

Tall did as he was told. The Boy climbed to the ground and stepped in front of Tall.

"Get down here," the Boy commanded.

Tall knelt down to one knee, closer to eye level with the Boy.

"Are you my pal, Tall?"

"Yes."

"Well, shit what kind of pal would I be to set you out just cause you endanger me? That's the best kind of friend to have. Figure it makes life real interesting."

"Interesting?"

"Shut your yap and listen. Now, I'm going to get

back on your shoulders, and me and you will let this thing blow over and we'll be back at home 'fore you know it. Deal?"

"Deal."

"Shake my hand, kind sir."

The boy reached out his hand with aristocratic flair. Tall accepted it, and the boy shook it with unusual vigor.

"All right. Glad that's settled."

The boy returned to Tall's shoulders and they continued north.

That night Tall cleared out a small cave while the boy built a fire inside of it. Before they slept that night, Tall gave the Boy a lesson about the One God. The boy found sleep quickly, as did Tall.

Tall dreamt of the Light most every night.

It always comforted him as he interpreted the dreams as a sign from the One God, that perhaps he would be permitted to enter the light with the full humans, and not the Depths like the Ogre Folk. His guardians had told him as a child that they were simply dreams, but Tall secretly defied their opinion. What sort of god would tease him in such a fashion? The One God was reaching out to Tall, telling him that there was a chance. He knew it would not be easy, but perhaps if he resisted his nature enough, if he lived the right life, the One God would find pity on him and save him from the Depths.

He awoke in the darkness, realizing the Boy was no longer by his side and that the fire had died out.

Tall came upon the camp. The remains of the Boy lay naked near ashes from their fire. Tall decided to not dwell on the damage to the Boy's body. He took him to a creek and washed him to the best of his ability, but grew angry when what remained of the Boy's entrails began to detach and flow downstream. Tall wrapped the Boy in the blanket the Woman had given him. Tall lay down and held the body close and wept in his sleep.

He did not dream.

He sprinted through the woods, toppling trees in his path, uncaring of the noise he was making. He no longer had to track by sight. The ogre folk were close enough that he could smell them. Tall gritted his teeth, ashamed at his need for rest and that he had given them any hope of escape.

He came upon them as they walked in a line, single file. They spun around to face him in unison, seven total, all prepared for a fight. Tall did not care about the element of surprise.

The last in line attempted to charge Tall, to match his savagery. It barked in a language Tall did not understand or ever care to learn. Its spear was clearly stolen from men, and was short for the ogre's stature. It hurled the spear at Tall, hoping to slow down the giant's gallop. Tall deflected the spear, snapping it with a swing of his forearm. Then Tall was upon the first ogre, biting into its throat with his rowed, barbed teeth, tasting the warm copper that was at once satisfying and infuriating. The ogre fell to its knees, eyes bulging as it placed its paws on its ruined throat.

The next two seemed to be brothers, both bearing an appearance that mirrored jackals. They drew bows in unison and took aim at Tall, who now shuffled towards them, blood falling from his grotesque chasm of a mouth, his teeth pushed out like ancient stalactites.

The Jackal Brothers concentrated and released their arrows, but Tall crossed his arms in front of his face and neck, and the arrows plunged into the meat of Tall's forearms. The dog men let out yips of distress, one replaced his arrow and took aim as the other drew his short sword.

Tall grabbed their heads and smashed them together, shattering their skulls, their faces forming into a patchwork Chimera of gore.

Tall snatched up one of the Jackal Brothers' swords and hurled it at an approaching ogre. The sword landed square in the stunned thing's chest, the blade shoved clear through his body, sending him off his feet.

The remaining three ran.

Tall was delighted. He had worried true Ogre folk were not capable of emotions, that they were mere animals living moment to moment.

These Ogres were prophets, though. For they had seen a vision of their fates. The Beast of the Sea had personally come to return them to the Depths.

He pursued them at a sprint, his stamina unfazed as the ogre folk were forced to slow. He reached out and managed to grab a tangle of an ogre's hair. Tall pulled him back with a yank, then braced its neck and jaw in his hands. He twisted and its head separated from its body. Tall howled as he pursued his remaining two enemies on all fours, unashamed of his true nature.

The two ogres left yipped and grunted at each other as they ran, and Tall hoped that they were devising a strategy of attack. He wanted to take them apart piece by piece in combat that had been denied him all of his life. He wanted them to see him in all of his glory, doing what he was born to do.

For the One God had stated that death was daily and so it was good.

In his blood lust, Tall had not noticed that the ogres were fleeing to a camp. He saw a couple of crude huts and a small dying fire not far in the distance. He saw humanoid movement there, and thought he would be adding more to his death toll.

The two ogres fell into the camp and began to bark orders. Tall slowed his pace. A few goblins strolled out of the huts, but at the sight of Tall the small humanoids ran the opposite direction into the forest. He allowed it.

One of the ogres went inside of a hut, while the other stood firm. The remaining ogre pulled out a human battle axe, which for him served as a one-handed hatchet. It snarled at Tall, issuing a pathetic last warning not to enter.

Tall rushed at the ogre, and it swung its hatchet sideways hoping for a neck blow, but Tall caught its arm in mid swing and bit into the ogre's bicep. The ogre stumbled back, stupefied. It stared in horror at the arm stump, as Tall had ripped its arm off with the bite. The ogre blubbered while Tall reached down to pick up the axe from the freshly severed hand. The ogre fell to its knees and did not resist Tall's killing blow, its skull split open from the axe.

The last one staggered out of the hut, leading a human girl on a leash. The ogre pushed the girl at Tall and put the leash in Tall's hand. It stroked her blond hair and grinned at Tall.

Tall snatched the ogre by its lower jaw and yanked back, and with a crunch it was cowering, holding its mouth where its jaw used to be. It sank to the ground, its tongue flopping about uselessly as blood spurt freely as a mocking, macabre celebration. Tall stomped his head to mush, but was not satisfied.

He turned to the girl.

She sobbed and fell at Tall's feet. She begged him not to take her, not to kill her.

Tall was disturbed that he did not feel pity for the girl.

"I will escort you to the edge of the forest," he said.

****

The Woman allowed him to bury the body with little fanfare in a grave near the creek bed where they had met. Tall covered it with stones while she sang to the One God. They returned to her home and she told him to come in and eat and warm himself by the hearth. He declined.

"There's still work to be done here. You can stay on as long as you like."

"I need to head on."

She nodded. "I'll pray for you, Tall. I'll pray for your soul."

He smiled, not bothering to conceal his teeth.

"I don't imagine I have a soul, ma'am," he said.

He turned as if to walk towards the path, but glanced back.

"But I appreciate the sentiment."

THE HORSE ALWAYS GETS IT FIRST

AXEL HOWERTON

"Drop the rifle, Whitley. We have you on all sides!" The echo carried the redcoat's Limey-tinged voice through the canyon like the thundering command of God himself.

Chester shuffled nervous at Whitley's back, shoes clattering on the dusty rock. Whitley cranked the lever on the Winchester and set it against his shoulder, aiming just above the voice coming from the other side of the gorge. It wouldn't do to kill a Mounted, especially not the Chief Constable. The crack of the shot was deafening, but the kick on this new rifle was more manageable than on his old Henry. The bullet sang as it sheared away a flake of shale just above the outcrop where the Mounties hid, exactly where he'd set his sights.

"Landsakes! How the hell did he hit that from there?" Sergeant Kendricks waved his men back from the outcrop and into the shade of the rock.

"Goddamn, sir. That must be two hundred yards, and I didn't see no smoke. Where the hell is he shooting from?"

"Out in the bloody canyon, that's where. Fall back." Kendricks shouted.

****

Whitley pulled the field glass from his pack and caught sight of red coats and white helmets scrambling down through the rocks, backing out onto the horse trail that led out of the canyon and back onto the plains.

"You see that Chester?" he laughed. "They ain't never seen the likes of this Winchester. I told you it was worth the twenty dollars."

He tucked the glass away and slid the rifle into its scabbard before taking the reins and pulling Chester's head into his chest, stroking the Tobiano's forehead and whispering quietly to calm him. The clattering stopped and Chester settled in to a quiet snuffling before shaking his head to loosen the dust from his matted mane.

Whitley cursed under his breath as he pulled back the tarp from the small cart they'd dragged--bouncing and crashing--through Horsethief Canyon, desperate to duck the damnable Mounted Police. Most of his stock was broken and left wasting in the dust. A careful inventory and a pile of broken glass had Whitley left with two full cases of brownish whiskey and six bottles of cloudy bug-juice, which looked as if someone had pissed in half-full jars of rotten fruit and dinner leavings. Moldy berries and hunks of tobacco floated in a greenish-yellow haze. The Bloods and the Crowfoot wouldn't care. They liked it just fine, the tobacco and coffee grounds gave it an extra kick, not to mention the laudanum haze that came from the drippings of a dozen whorehouse castaway bottles. It didn't really matter what you put in that shit, the Indians would drink it.

Eighteen bottles was a piss-poor drop from the twenty crates he'd left Fort Benton with, but it was better than a bullet, or a stretch in the cells at Fort Hamilton. The Mounteds had set upon him as he bartered with a clutch of Blackfoot braves a good fifty miles back. They would have scouted back and found his camp, either the Reds or the redskins. Either way, the rest of his stock would be gone. Those bottles would have netted him twenty or thirty buffalo robes, which Whitley would have shipped out East for a reasonable sum. It wasn't retirement money, but if he was shrewd, it would keep him in good stead for a meager winter. Now he'd be lucky to salvage enough to buy a bottle of real whiskey to keep himself warm. It surely stung to have lost the entire run. He'd brought it all the way up from the Missouri, through the Indian country, snuck it into the Alberta territories, up the Whoop-Up trail, and all the way to the Blackfoot Crossing without breaking a single damned bottle.

"Goddammit, Chester," he moaned, "we got us in a hellspot, boy."

Chester whinnied in reply and kicked a hoof against the rock.

"I know, we're sorely bit this time."

Whitley hit the dirt as the whistle cut the air. The first shell landed wide, disintegrating an outcrop thirty feet to their left, but shaking the ground beneath their feet, setting Chester bucking and scrabbling at the edge of the rocky slope.

"Whoa! Chester!" Whitley dove for the reins and pulled his horse back away from the embankment. "You're gonna take yourself straight down to hell, you damned fool!"

"Again!" Kendricks shouted from somewhere in the clouds of dust that had risen all around them. "I want that Union criminal buried under this canyon, by God!" Then calling out to Whitley, "Did that one finish you Whitley? You miserable, disease-ridden rat!"

The second shell hit true, exploding in a shower of limestone and shale, throwing Whitley from his feet, stray shards of rock flying fast as bullets, pounding against his back and creasing his scalp where his hat gave no protection.

Chester panicked against the shifting shale, scrabbling backwards as the ground slid away beneath him. The cart twisted and jack-knifed around the side of the horse, pulled away from what was left of the makeshift hitch, and tumbled over the rocks, spilling the last of the boxes out into the ravine, crashing to the canyon floor, as the horse began to lose its footing.

"Shit! Piss! Sonofawhore!" Whitley cried out, scrambling to

his feet and past the bewildered horse, sliding down the slope in a cloud of dust and profanity. Chester high-stepped, one hoof at a time, nervously picking his way down after his master like a far better trained animal.

Further and further down into the canyon, Whitley's voice echoed back up into the empty sky, foul words repeated endlessly with the clicking and clamoring of falling rocks like an endless game of billiards from farther and farther away.

The shells continued to explode above them, the crumbled remains of the canyon raining down on them as they picked their way to the bottom of the ravine.

Kendricks voice continued to ring out, laughing now, urging his men to drop more hellfire upon them, to bury the whiskey runner at the bottom of the world.

Whitley hit the canyon floor on his knees, sobbing as he crawled towards the broken remains of the cart.

"Aww, Chester. You stupid, shit-brained horse. What the hell did you do, you sonofabitching bastard!"

Chester came clopping down into the bottom of the canyon sideways, hoof over hoof, a miracle of pure willpower that would have killed or broken any other horse. Whitley was on his knees, covered with red dust, face lined with sweat and blood, digging through the glass with bloody fingers, cursing Kendricks and Chester with every breath. He finally lifted one bottle—one last untouched bottle of murky gold—as if it were a baby, cradling it in his arms.

"One. One goddamn bottle, Chester. I oughta beat you to death. And then beat you some more when you're dead. Goddamn you, Chester. Goddamn you."

For his part, Chester stood stoic and silent, scraping one shoe against the rock under his feet.

****

Dark came fast in the bottom of the canyon, but the broken crates and the remains of the cart gave ample fuel for the fire. Whitley poured the last of the water from his canteen into a pot for Chester, then sat with his back to the horse, cradling the last of his whiskey, face red and eyes watering, whether from the fire, or the drink or the desperate feeling of absolute destruction, he couldn't tell. Whitley knew the score of the game. He had lost. Bad. Stuck at the bottom of a rocky canyon, the path blown to smithereens. No water, no food, no purpose and no hope. All he had left was the whiskey, which would not last him out the night. If they didn't freeze by morning, the temperature would rise and they'd be cooked alive before they could find their way out or climb their way up, especially the horse.

"Chester," he called out, to the night more than the horse. "Looks like we're done in."

Whitley stood and dusted himself off and picked the bottle from the ground. He strode to where Chester stood, licking at the pot, regarding him for a moment before he shook his head and laughed. "Well, you old sonofabitch, looks like you're all the lousy excuse for company I got left. Might as well have us a drink."

Whitley took an extra shirt from his pack and set to filtering out the half bottles and small puddles he could collect, wringing out what would have been two, two-and-a-half bottles of bug juice into Chester's pot.

He'd only seen a drunk horse once before, but it had been a sight to behold and there were worse ways to spend your last night on Earth. Chester sniffed at the pot as Whitley patted the horse gently on the neck.

"Alright then."

The next hours were filled with laughter echoing through the canyon, as Whitley stoked the fire with the liquor-soaked remains of his cart and slowly succumbed to drink, watching Chester, kicking and dancing, stumbling from side to side and whinnying like a horse half his age, before they both fell into the careless slumber of a whiskey drunk.

****

Whitley awoke to the sun bright overhead, the high rock walls trapping in the heat. It was near noon, and the temperature had risen to a sweltering hellfire. Chester was nudging him towards the dark edge of the canyon floor.

113

Whitley slowly clawed his way out of the stupor, spitting what might be the last of his moisture out with a mouthful of dust before taking his knees and then his feet.

"Alright, alright, goddammit. I didn't mean to tell you this way, but there ain't no hope for us, Chester. We`re gonna die down here, we might as well sit and be comfortable."

It wasn't until Chester had nearly forced him to the wall that he noticed the glint of metal from one shaded crevasse in the rock.

"What the Sam Hell is that?"

Chester neighed and led the way, creeping slowly around an almost invisible corner.

"How did we not see this last night?" Whitley mumbled as he followed his horse into the shadows. The further they stepped into the alcove, the more blessedly cool it became.

The cave they found themselves in was filled with light. Whitley had never seen so much metal in one place. It was rounded and huge, a silver egg as big as a house. It was a strange ore, highly polished and oddly vibrant. It gleamed in the darkness as if lit from within. Whitley ran his hands around the smooth concave surface, marveling at how cool and pure and seamless it was beneath his fingers. Chester stood back, neck rigid and head turned to keep the massive object locked in one wide staring eye.

"Hells Bells, Chester! What do you suppose this thing is? Must be worth a damned fortune!" Whitley whistled as he ducked beneath and examined the strange legs holding the egg from the floor of the cave.

"I'll be good and goddamned!"

Chester bucked and backed towards the wall as a pop and hiss broke the silence.

Whitley jumped back, tumbling out onto the ground clear of the weird egg-machine, eyes bulging as a seam appeared across the side of the thing, turning at corners and running parallel to reveal a rectangular section that moved away from the whole, floating down across the surface and exposing a doorway to the innards of whatever-the-hell this was.

Whitley sat in the dust, jaw wide and lips trembling.

Chester crowded himself into one dim corner, muscles tense and head down, ready to run, even with nowhere to go. The horse shuffled in place, hooves cracking against the floor, and protested loudly as Whitley's curiosity won out against caution. Chester watched with one wild eye, as his master disappeared into the glowing doorway of the metal thing.

Whitley stepped inside the weird metal cave, bewildered as the very metal of the walls and ceiling and floor began to glow with their own strange luminescence. Whitley had seen something of the sort on the beach near Fort San Luis Ray, where he had gone for a skinny-dip with a pretty Mexican whore one hot August night. The crystal jellyfish had swarmed in on the tide and lined up a mile down the beach, flashing with their crazy blue light like stars fallen to the sand. This was even more curious. The chamber opened up, beyond what should have been possible, given the objects outer dimensions. As Whitley took one trepidatious step after another, the light glowing from the room around him moved as he moved, brightest where he stood, darkest at the farthest edges of the space. The strange metal of the thing seemed formed to purpose, flowing out into shelves and desks and rising up from the floor like tree-stumps just in places where a man might be likely to sit at one of the protruding areas near the one side, what Whitley felt impelled to think of as the front. Whitley had seen a few sights in his time. Once he had been to London— the real London, the original London, the one in England— and he'd seen a horseless cart pushed by steam, like a train. This was different though—newer, yet older—it had that feeling of a long-abandoned camp. No noise of cogs and gears and steam pipes bursting with power. No coal-fire warmth, no action to create a reaction. The place felt as quiet and lonely as a tomb. Ghosts lived here, and ghosts alone.

From outside the room Chester whinnied. Whitley started at the sound, but he knew Chester well enough.

"I'm fine, dammit. Just calm yourself, horse."

He could hear Chester clomping in the dust, nervous to be

near this thing. Whitley stepped carefully toward one of the desks formed from the wall, ran his hand gently over the bejeweled surface, dozens of tiny, twinkling lights coming to life at his touch. A new light began to glow in a square on the wall in front of him. A frame with no picture. A window with no view. Strange symbols, illuminated in a soft green ember, rose against the darkening wall. The symbols flickered and changed, running lengthwise in a seemingly endless procession. Whitley touched a finger to the wall, running it across the odd magic window in the wall, watching the symbols fade and reappear as his finger touched and retouched the glittering characters.

Suddenly, the lights rose to a full noon brightness and the thing came alive, rumbling from beneath him and unleashing a strange vibration like a rail rattling with an oncoming train. Whitley stumbled back, covering his eyes from the glare, tripping over himself until his back was at the back wall from the moving picture and the glittering desk. Whitley yelped as the wall fell away and he tumbled into an entirely new room, where the surroundings already burned hot and white.

He stood and dusted his pants with trembling hands as he took in his new surroundings. Like the first chamber, this one seemed to be made entirely of the strange metal, molded and shaped without flaw, desks, shelves and what must be wardrobes and cupboards growing from the walls. The middle of the room was taken up by a large table, set at a strange angle, the one end low to the ground and the other about elbow height for Whitley. A strange mechanism hung from the ceiling. It was the first thing he'd seen in this place that didn't merge with everything else. It was terrible and foreboding, some kind of instrument of torture with spears and gun barrels poking out at the end, an array of tubes and wires cascading down and leading to one of the desk areas, where more of the twinkling jewels lined the tabletop. Keeping wide of the dangling machine, Whitley stepped slowly towards the wardrobes, marveling at the smoky glass doors, cautiously reaching, wondering at the lack of handles and knobs. There were precious few things in this place that seemed meant for human hands.

He paused, wringing his hands, saying goodbye to his fingers, just in case they didn't make it back with the rest of his hand. He fumbled at the sliver of space between the doors, finding purchase and prying open the front of the cabinet.

Rows of strange containers lined the shelves, holding bits of floating carcass and ephemera, some of it familiar—a seashell, an acorn, what looked like a cow's eyeball—some of it so completely foreign that Whitley could scarcely conceive of what they might have once been—spider-like creatures with twelve or more legs, all twisting the wrong way of any crawler he'd ever seen; a three-foot worm with a gaping round maw full of razor-teeth and finger-like appendages running down both sides of its body; a pair of bull balls? No. Bull balls were bigger and darker. These looked like...

Whitley realized his fingers were held snug around his own berries and loosened his grip, wiping his sleeve at his face, suddenly reacquainted with the thirst that had been gnawing at him since he woke. Swallowing the dry lump at the back of his throat, Whitley set to pulling the other cabinets open, one by one, rifling the contents for something to drink. Most of the containers were full of oddities, like the first shelves, a few of them recognizable bits of a man. The thirst was strong enough to ward off any thoughts of what that might mean about the owners of this place, and Whitley searched on, finally coming upon a single metal tube that sloshed in his hands and did not offer a view into some queer creature or the excised bits of one. It looked not unlike an artillery shell, but smooth and silver. No telling what might be inside the thing.

Whitley worked his hands around it, looking for some sign of a lid or a clasp and finding none. He stumbled back out into the main chamber, cursing under his breath. He flung the tube out into the dirt and stepped out after it, kicking the damnable thing off towards Chester, who side-stepped in a panic and shook his head in affront.

"Dirty whore!"

Whitley squatted in the dust and put his face in his hands.

"We're gonna die in this canyon."

Chester brayed and put his muzzle to the floor, knocking the tube back towards Whitley with a swipe of his head.

"What?"

Chester huffed and stepped carefully towards the open door of the egg, nodding his head up and down towards it.

"What? You want me to take it back in there? It can sit like shit on the floor for all I care."

Chester continued to grumble and nod.

"What goddammit? What?"

As if the horse could understand him, Chester pointed his muzzle down at the thing at Whitley's feet, then threw his head up at the door one last time. Whitley shook his head in exasperation and picked up the tube, ready to hurl it either at the horse or the egg.

"We're gonna die down here, and you're worried about if I put this thing back where I got..."

Whitley trailed off as the now familiar pop and hiss sounded off in his hand, watching in amazement as clear liquid began to pour to the ground.

"Sonofabitch!"

Whitley righted the bottle, grasping it tight with both hands, silently praying over the contents, even as he sniffed at the liquid inside. He dipped two fingers into the opening, bringing them out moist and sniffing closer before letting two drops fall upon his dry and cracked lips. He then dipped the fingers again, this time cramming them greedily into his mouth before taking a swig straight from the open mouth of the bottle.

His laughter boomed through the small cavern.

"Holy heavens and praise the goddamn Lord above, Chester! We're saved!"

Whitley sprang to his feet and raced out of the cave, returning quickly with Chester's pot, which he set in front of the horse and carefully poured the water into.

Chester put his nostrils down into the iron pot and snuffed quickly, three times, pausing before he began to lap at what

Whitley had given him.

Whitley himself took another swallow from the container and began to dance a happy little jig, still laughing.

A strange twitch began to manifest itself through Whitley's body, like too much coffee or not enough sleep. It began in his chest, his heart fluttering like a bird, and moved into his muscles as he began to convulse with an inner chill so forceful that he dropped the strange bottle and collapsed to his knees.

He tried to call out a warning to Chester, feeling a mad panic grip his brain as sound and vision merged into one kaleidoscopic madness, the cave around him swirling into more colors than he had ever known existed. Whitley felt his body hit the ground. He knew he was locked in a fit of tremors, he could see it, as if he was standing outside of himself, watching his body twitch and revolt.

"Poison! Poison!" rang through his head like cannon fire, impossibly loud and forceful. But it wasn't his voice, it was a low, hoarse voice, but full of the terror he felt bolting through his own body.

"Poison! Dying! Whitley!"

Whitley—spirit Whitley—standing outside of himself like a ghost, felt a mighty blast as if that cannonade had finally come to rest, a colossal ball of iron thudding into the ground in front of him, throwing him tumbling backwards through empty air. Then nothing. Black. He was dead.

Of course if he was dead, where in the hell where the calling angels and the gates of Heaven?

Whitley struggled to remember, forcing himself to see the body twitching on the floor, to look to Chester, lying next to him, foam on his muzzle, head lying in a pool of the strange liquid that had proved their undoing.

Slowly he felt himself fading back into his own body, as if ethereal hands had scooped him from his ghostly resting place and was setting him, gently, back into the body that had loosed him.

He could once again feel himself, flesh and blood, around his consciousness. His muscles tingled with some bizarre energy, tickling on the inside, filled with unfocused purpose, unused fuel. He was invigorated as he'd never felt before. It was like boyhood birthday mornings, waiting for his special breakfast from his Mama. It was like his first time with a woman. His first time wallowing in whiskey. All at once and all on top of each other. Whitley felt more full of spit than he'd ever felt in his miserable life. The sudden return of his faculties set him bolt upright, sitting in the dirt of the cave, eyes wide and heart racing, a wide, manic smile pulling at the corners of his face.

"Holy Hell! Goddamn and sonofabitch!" He hollered, leaping to his feet like a spring—heeled goat.

He pounced on Chester, laughing and tugging at the horse's mane.

"Come on goddamn it! Chester! Wake up, you lazy sack of blue meat!"

"WHITLEY!" The voice boomed again, deep and resonant.

Whitley fell back on his ass, stunned. He clapped his hands to his ears, but the voice came again, unmuffled and just as thunderous.

"WHITLEY!"

"Sweet Jesus! Who is that? Stop the goddamn yelling!"

Chester shook beneath him and jolted up from the floor in one fluid movement, bucking and turning circles in the dust, as agitated as Whitley had ever seen him.

"WHITLEY! WHITLEY!" Came the panicked voice again, so loud and terrifying that it might shake down the cave around them.

Except there wasn't a tremor. Not a grain of dust out of place in the cavern, Whitley realized. And no echo. Hadn't there been a terrific echo when Chester had been braying at him from out here in the cave?

Despite the thunderstorm of that voice, Whitley forced his hands away from his ears and grabbed the bridle, pulling Chester's cheek to his chest, flicking the forelock away and firmly stroking the blaze marking that ran his forehead, top to bottom as he'd done since the horse was a feisty colt.

As Whitley hushed the horse, he was glad of the booming voice receding, softening to a reasonable level, although it still came intermittently, mumbling his name.

With the horse calmed, Whitley stepped away and around the cave, searching for some hidden nook or cranny that might hide some bastard with a trumpet, shouting out his name, some damned Mounted toying with them before striking.

"Who the hell is in here?" Whitley called out, his voice clattering in the corners and returning to him. "The hell? Ain't that curious?"

"Whitley. We need to leave this place." No echo. Bouncing inside his head like a remembered conversation.

"What the good goddamn?" Whitley shook his head, hoping to bust it loose and free himself from this odd feeling of intrusion in his mind, like a second person walking around in his brains.

Chester nudged him from behind, drawing his attention and pointing his muzzle down at the water pot on the floor. At the same time, the voice came again.

"Whitley. Bad water. We need to leave here. This is a bad place. Bad place. Whitley."

The words popped into his head as reminiscences, like someone trying to pluck the right words from his memory. Chester nudged again and Whitley stared into the horse's watery eye.

"Chester?"

The vision opened up in Whitley's mind like a daydream, a simple vision of a spring meadow, Whitley sitting on a blanket under a tree, a lovely senorita beside him, her dress fanned out around her, caramel ankles peeking out beneath, crossed demurely, but lovely bare feet open to the breeze. Whitley remembered that day, the last day with Rosita before he left for Montana. Rosita stood and laughed, throwing her long, dark hair behind her with a flip of her sweet head, as she picked up an apple from the basket and walked toward him. Not him. He was still lying back on the blanket, propped on an elbow, watching the sway of Rosita's hips as she walked away from him. Yet here she was, holding out the apple to his eyes. Not his eyes. Chester's.

"What the shit!"

Back in the cave, Whitley tripped backwards over himself, ass-over-teakettle into the dirt. Staring up at his horse, mind reeling.

"Whitley?" The voice in his head repeated. "We need to leave. Now. Whitley."

It was Chester. Chester was inside his head, he could hear him. What's more, Whitley was in Chester's head, seeing his memories, feeling his fear.

"The bad water, Whitley. I hear you. Inside."

Whitley scrambled back on his ass, until his back hit rock.

"Get outta my goddamned head, Chester!"

"Whitley. We have to leave here. This is a bad place. Bad water. We need good water. Fresh. Water."

Whitley wailed and crawled out of the cave, back into the canyon, the heat blasting him in the face as he hit the open air, the noon sun staring directly down on them now. The ground was blistering hot.

Whitley pawed at the dirt, rolled to his back, curling into a ball. Surely he was losing his mind. Maybe they had always been lying in the bottom of this canyon. Baking in the heat, dying in a fever dream. That's what it was, a fever dream, the last wavering insanity of a broken man, cooking in his own skin at the very depths of hell on Earth.

"Just take me, you bastards! Just take me!"

Chester stepped out into the sun, wincing at the light after so long in the darkness of the cave. He stared down at Whitley, moaning and cursing in the dirt.

"Get up, you stupid man." Chester willed Whitley up off the ground and was mildly surprised to see him lift up off of the ground, exactly as he willed it. Whitley struggled, arms and legs kicking out all akimbo, as he was heaved into the air by invisible hands.

"What the shit! What the shit! Put me down, you goddamn devils!"

Chester focused harder, already feeling the power welling inside of his mind, knowing he could control things he could never have understood before. Whitley slowly floated up into empty space, feet lifting off of the earth until he was raised up and over Chester's head, set down clumsily on his withers and sliding down into place on his back. Whitley grasped at Chester's mane and yanked, hard.

"OW! BASTARD!" Chester bellowed, at which Whitley let go of the mane and clamped his hands over his ears, sliding to the side and tumbling off the horse, landing hard on his side in the dust.

"Jesus Christ, Chester! Not so loud!" He caterwauled into the ether between them.

Chester, at the shouting in his own newly-sensitive head, clattered and spun, throwing his head to the sky with a whinny and another cry in his mind.

"SHIT!"

"Balls!"

"OW! BASTARD!"

"Fucking horse! Knock it off!"

"OW! STOP! WHITLEY!"

"Shit Hell! Chester!"

Whitley finally gained his feet, hands still clamped to his ears, ducking and running for shelter from the horse, now stomping and bucking like a wild beast. Whitley ran to the far wall of the canyon, where he cried out once more, wishing he had something to throw at the damned devil animal. As if answering his prayer, a handful of stones rocketed from the dirt and fired towards Chester.

"SHIT! OW!" Fresh missiles launched from around Chester's feet, several striking true and knocking Whitley back to the ground.

Whitley stood, facing away from his attacker, all thought of retaliation faded.

"Chester," he said, natural voice croaking out, stale and dry.

Another pellet bounced off of his temple, crumpling him to his knees.

"Knock it off, Goddammit! Look!" Whitley whined, holding his now bleeding head in one hand and pointing toward the slope with the other.

Chester bucked once more, then let go his hold on several rocks floating in the air around him, which clattered to the ground, raising a cloud of dust around him. He stepped carefully and warily towards Whitley, coming to a stop next to him and turning his head to regard what Whitley had found.

The trail was small, rocky, a natural cut in the rock that may not have led anywhere much, let alone out of the canyon, but it was hope. It was tucked behind an outcrop and invisible under shadow of night, but there it was. Salvation.

Whitley laughed.

Chester felt the joy of it, the relief, and matched it with his own. The two, man and horse, stood in a shared bewildering joy, laughing like old friends, all thoughts of death and hopelessness forgotten.

Whitley broke off and ran like a wild idiot to pack up camp. Stuffing what meager belongings they had left into the saddlebags and pack. Chester stood watching him until Whitley shambled over with the saddle.

"What are you doing?"

"Packing. What does it look like, y'idiot?"

"Not on my back. Not again." Chester declared coldly.

"Well I can't carry it all. You're the goddamn horse. That's your job. Horse."

Whitley grabbed the old, worn saddle and made to sling it over Chester's back, but instead found himself careening off of an invisible wall, falling backwards with the weight of the saddle. He dropped it into the dust and stood, indignant, staring into Chester's eye.

"I can't rightly ride without the saddle, can I?"

"No."

"Chester…"

Whitley stumbled back, taken with another vision from Chester's mind, the Negro market in Tallahassee, where they'd sauntered past a line of slaves, beaten and humiliated, broken men. Marched out of the city in chains, shouldering heavy loads and trodding the hard earth with their bare feet blistered and bleeding.

"You ain't no negro. You ain't no man. You're a goddamn horse, Chester. That's what God made you for, to carry shit and keep me running."

"No."

"Quit being stubborn, you sonofabitch, or I'll put you down."

Chester lifted him off of his feet again, then dropped him hard. The saddle floated over Whitley where he lay, then slammed down on top of his back, pinning him to the ground.

"Let me up, you dirty whore!"

"No."

Whitley struggled beneath the leather trap, to no avail.

"Get off me!"

"You carry it."

"Chester!"

Chester relented, releasing the saddle from his grip and lifting Whitley to his feet, setting him standing uneasy, but on both boot heels.

"Stop doing that, you asshole!" Whitley rushed at the horse with a fist raised, but thought better of it at the pain in his back where the saddle had hit him.

"Stop calling me names. I am no slave, Whitley."

"I guess you ain't no more, anyhow." Whitley stomped off to finish carrying the bags back.

Chester glared up the small trail, trying to divine just where it lead, and what the chances were that it would get them out of the canyon.

Whitley returned, seemingly humbled, and stood silently, waiting for Chester to acknowledge him.

"How'd you do that?" he asked quietly.

"What?"

"Tossing me around like a baby doll."

"You can do it too. You threw the rocks..."

Whitley stood, dumbfounded, staring down at the rocks at

his feet.

"Make it a dream in your mind." Chester said quietly.

Whitley pictured the rocks moving, floating in the air, swirling about him, the way they had for Chester. He stared, and stared. And stared. He thought he saw one of them tumble a bit to the left, but nothing else.

"Try harder." Chester mumbled inside his head.

Whitley stood there, fists clenched, dripping wet in the hot sun, pushing against the inside of his skull so hard that it began to ache like a two-bottle hangover. Move, goddammit! Move! When he finally let go of the breath he held in his chest, the only thing that had moved was the sweat rolling down his back.

"Bullshit!" he hollered, kicking the rocks at his feet. Whitley shouldered the pack and his Winchester, and left the saddlebags in the dust next to the saddle. He stomped past Chester and onto the trail, steadying himself with one hand as he clambered up between the rocks.

"Whitley?" Chester called after him, neighing loudly at the same time, a strange confluence of sound and thought.

"I'll carry this pile of misery," Whitley shouted back, "You want that there, you can bring it yourself. Goddamn useless horse."

Chester nodded towards the saddlebags, watching silently as they floated up and over him, waggling his head from side to side to settle them in place as they came to rest on his withers. He shifted them to rest in front of his barrel, in exactly the place that was most comfortable, something Whitley had never managed in ten years of fitting his tack.

Whitley picked his way up the trail, struggling to stay well ahead of Chester, who had now taken to simply floating himself over any outcrop or bramble too difficult. The only noise between them was an occasional clatter of hoof, and Whitley's mumbled cursing.

When they came to the crest of the canyon, the sun was almost on the horizon, and the clouds had taken the orange hue of coming evening. Chester set his newly keen eyes across the plains beneath them, seeking out the tiny river that girded the canyons.

"There," Chester pointed with his long face, exhaling a plume of dust from his nostrils as he nodded in the direction they needed to go.

Whitley dropped the pack and flopped down on top of it, landing squarely on the handle of his cookpot.

"Goddammit all to hell!"

Chester shook the dust from his mane and huffed again.

"Why are you so angry, Whitley?"

Whitley crossed his arms and dropped his head, hiding beneath the brim of his hat.

"Whitley?"

Whitley jabbed a hand towards the horse, extending some signal that Chester didn't understand, but the emotion came through loud and clear.

"Whitley. We need water. Real water."

Whitley shifted on the pack, turning his back to Chester, and wincing as he rolled over some other uncomfortable bit of equipment. Whitley pulled the Winchester from beneath him and tossed it aside.

"Whitley."

Chester clomped over and buried his nose in Whitley's back, nudging hard. Whitley responded only by tightening the grip on his own shoulders.

"WHITLEY!"

"Jesus H. Christ!" Whitley bellowed, jumping from his nest in the pack and stumbling away. The loose rocks beneath his feet began to shift as he got closer to the edge of the outcrop. Chester watched him slide away, a look of astonishment on Whitley's face as he began to wave his arms in the air like a bird, before disappearing into the dusk.

Whitley squeezed his eyes shut tight. He could feel his heart exploding into his ears as the wind whistled past and the ground rushed up to crush him in its grasp. It seemed like an eternity, terrified that the very second he opened his eyes would be the moment that he would explode against the dry earth.

He could hear rocks falling around him, crackling as they bounced against each other, a clickety-clackety symphony of gravity and danger. Then a strange snorting laughter, inhuman noises that danced in his head with joy and excitement. Chester. Chester was laughing at him. He was lying dead on the ground, a ghost, a specter of his life, and the goddamn horse was...

"Whitley! You did it!" Chester snorted.

Whitley ventured to open an eye and looked straight down into the dust, a half a foot away from his face. He was floating, hovering, inches away from death.

"Put me down, you asshole."

"I'm not doing it. You are."

Whitley closed his eyes again and pictured himself upright, plucked up by an invisible hand and set right on his boots in the very spot that nearly claimed him. He felt the solid ground beneath his feet and opened his eyes.

"Sonofabitch!"

They walked for an hour, forgetting themselves in chatter and fanciful bounds and leaps through the air and, once out of the foot of the canyons, they struck upon a small stream that led out the mile or so to the Red Deer River. Full of water and in the cooler clime of the prairie grass and lush trees that lined the riverbank, Whitley and Chester were recharged. Chester had been grazing here and there on the small patches of grass, but Whitley's stomach began to protest its lack of feeding.

"Godammit, I'm starvin'!"

Whitley scanned the trees and brush for berries, greens, some sort of animal he could quick roast to quell the cramping pain in his gut. His eyes finally fell on the middle of the river, where the telltale ripples of a fish played just beneath the surface. Whitley stomped to the riverbank, pulling his boots off and splashing into the water still rolling his pants at the knees.

"Whitley? What are you doing?"

"Catching me a damn fish, what's it look like?"

Chester laughed, and Whitley splashed back toward shore, furious.

"Why in the hell are you laughing at me again? Stupid goddamn horse! I gotta eat too! I can't eat no scrub grass and dry wheat!"

The fish came from nowhere, splattering down into the dirt, sputtering and flopping against the air.

Whitley jumped back, stumbling and splashing back on his ass in the water, suddenly submerged to his chest.

"Shit-hell! Thanks for nothin'!"

Chester closed his eyes, mustering his willpower and visualized Whitley slowly rising out of the water, hovering with his toes dangling just above the surface, and pictured him moving, ever so carefully, to dry land.

Whitley stared down past his dripping feet to the three little Western Goldeyes still gasping and twitching beneath him in the mud.

"Careful now."

The sound of his voice proved to break Chester's concentration, and Whitley dropped, the fish exploding beneath his feet as he thudded to the ground.

"Shitheels!"

Chester laughed again, neighing and high stepping despite himself.

"Damn you, Chester!" Whitley grumbled, gingerly stepping back to the water to wash his feet.

Whitley looked back to the shore with a look of concern.

"Aww. Goddammit. Didn't you bring the packs when I fell off the goddamn cliff back there?"

"I did not. I was concerned about your fall."

"You forgot. All the damned cookpots was in there. Aww. Jesus. What about the rifle? The Winchester? That cost me twenty goddamn dollars!"

"We will return for it after you have eaten and rested."

"Damnation."

****

A half-hour later the rest of the fish had been salvaged and roasted over a small fire with a stripling Whitley had ripped from a nearby tree. The meal devoured, Whitley sat, picking his teeth with the branch.

"Them's better smoked or fried, but beggars can't be choosers, I guess."

"Smells terrible."

"You ain't had eatin,' till you've had smoked fish and that soft French cheese."

Chester made an odd guttural sound that came across in Whitley's head with a wave of nausea.

"How come you're so much better at this stuff than me?" Whitley asked, shaking his head, "and you being a goddamned horse?"

"My mind seems calmer than yours. You are always distracted with so many thoughts and memories and things that aren't real."

"That's what a mind is. You ignoramus."

"And so much anger if you aren't the center of attention."

"Hey now! Watch it!" Whitley poked the air with his fingers, "You're still the horse, and I'm the man. According to the bible, you ain't but a beast of burden, set here to make my life easier."

"That's what you make of me. I've never known any different until today. I was born into work for men. Now my mind is free. I am free."

"Don't that beat all? You calling yourself a slave again? You ain't no slave, dummy. You're a damned horse."

"A horse that has helped, and shared, and saved your life. More than once."

Whitley tossed the stick aside. "Are you talking about yesterday? Because you're the one got us stuck in that godforsaken pit. I had everything under control until you done got spooked and fell down the canyon and smashed the shit out of our payload."

"You see? Our payload."

"Fuck you, horse. My payload. All this crazy horseshit? Your fault."

"We are friends, Whitley. Partners."

"We ain't nothin' but an asshole, and the asshole what rides on his back."

Whitley spat and went back to staring out across the river, as he listened to Chester picking his way off through the brush.

"Asshole." Whitley mumbled into his beard.

He sat, shoulders slumped, head bowed against the sun, for the better part of a quarter hour before his rage had passed. Whitley stood and dusted his pants, straightened his hat and looked down at the rocks at his feet. He shot a quick glance around him in the trees to be sure that damnable horse wasn't watching, waiting to lord over him if he failed. Whitley held his hand out, palm down as he closed his eyes to concentrate. Slowly, trembling against the edge of his boot, three stones clacked against each other before rising slowly in the air. He jumped when he felt the rocks press against his outstretched hand, snapping his fist shut around them before carefully opening his hand to inspect his reward.

"Well, goddamn!"

Whitley shuffled a quick jig in the dirt and laughed. "Chester! Hey, Chester! I did it!"

The weight of his misery, realizing Chester wasn't waiting in the shadows, cemented his feet, and the rocks suddenly felt unbearably tiny inside his hand.

Whitley felt a new wave of anger fill his body and his arm flew before he'd even considered it, the pebbles skipping across the surface of the river, landing with a splash.

The explosion knocked him off of his feet, the torrent hitting him like a hurricane as it lashed out from the river.

Stunned, Whitley rolled back towards the trees.

"Whitley! Come on out here, you bastard!"

Kendricks.

The zing of bullets slicing the air was followed by branches shearing off of the trees where he had been standing a moment before. Where the hell where they? Whitley knew they couldn't possibly hit him from that far with their useless old stock rifles, unless…

Whitley fell back further, crouching at the tree-line, searching the surrounding hills for the source of the voice, and the shots that had nearly killed him.

"Whitley! Turn yourself over and I might not kill you outright." Kendrick shouted, braying like a hyena in between threats.

Whitley heard the gunpowder explode, and the whine of the second volley with just enough time to leap a few yards further into the bush before the crack of the cannonball leveled a birch next to where he'd been standing. Now he knew where they were, but he didn't have the Winchester. He also didn't have a horse to ride out on. Where in the hell had Chester gone?

Whitley dodged his way through the stand of trees, weaving in and around, praying that Kendricks men miscalculated how fast he could play hopscotch through the woods. Panic turned to blind fear as he ran, hearing more explosions to his left, and then his right. Now feeling as if he was moving faster in his mind, in his own eyes, than his body was actually running. The trees began to bend and bow out of his way, cracking here and there, as he felt his feet leave the solid earth and flail helplessly in the air.

"Chester! Goddamn it, Chester!" he caterwauled into the green blur.

The trees gave way to scrub, which gave way to the dirt and red clay of the foot of the canyons. Whitley stumbled and rolled, tumbling out into the plain.

Whitley lay, confused and spent, eyes shooting in all directions before realizing how far he'd come, that he was far out of range of the cannon, and the rifle, probably out of range of Kendricks' field glass for that matter. He'd somehow been thrown—pulled—flown at least four miles, and was now resting atop one of the hills on the opposite ridge, looking down at the canyons

"Goddamn it Chester! You almost killed..."

Whitley sat up, puzzled.

"Chester?"

He was alone, dusk settling in over the top of the paint-striped hills, the orange and purple tinge of dusk veiled by a gathering darkness of storm clouds, already coming down on the far-side of the range, hopefully right on top of Kendricks and his damned Mounteds.

Whitley gazed out at the majesty of the view, realizing finally that Chester had not pulled his bacon out of the fire. He had done it himself—he, Emerson Whitley, lousy rotgut runner and perpetual failure—had flown through the air like a bird, faster than a galloping stallion. A smile crossed his face and he once again felt the strange loneliness of being without his horse. His friend. Chester was right about that. He'd gotten Whitley out of more scrapes than he could count, and he'd been a constant and undeservedly loyal companion for longer than Whitley could fathom.

He stood tall, closed his eyes and took a deep breath, focusing all of his newfound power and reaching out from inside of his mind, across the vast expanse that lay open to him where only his memories used to be.

Chester? He called out. Chester?

Then he saw him, carelessly clomping back along the path they'd been on before they stopped at the riverside. He was looking through Chester's eyes as the horse broke the trees and stepped out on to the river bank, stepping carefully towards it before dipping his head to the water to drink. Memory? Had Chester drank when they were at the river? He must have. But the light. The light was fading. Chester's gaze turned to the trees, marking the splintered remains and ravaged stumps left in the wake of...

No!

The hot blaze of fear and anger filled his head again, accompanied by one single fierce need.

He felt the air rush past him, and dared not open his eyes. Whitley prayed harder than he'd ever prayed, willed himself against his own life, to be there, to save Chester, to...

The terrible motion stopped, like running at a full drunken sprint into the side of a barn. Whitley felt himself lying on cold, hard earth and forced his eyes open. He was back, in the trees, mere yards from the river. Chester lay in a heap out in the open, and Whitley could hear Kendricks yelling out to his troops.

"Get down there, you sons of bitches!"

Whitley crawled, careful and quiet, out to where Chester lay in the dirt. "Chester," he whispered, before realizing the futility of using his now-obsolete vocal chords.

"Chester?" he reached out through the darkness in his mind.

"Whitley?"

"Praise the lord! You alright, Chester?"

"Whitley?"

Whitley crawled toward Chester, careful to move slowly and keep low to the ground.

Crawling around to face Chester, Whitley paused as his knees found a thick pool of blood beneath them.

"Aww, shit, Chester."

"Whitley. Is it night already? I feel cold. Whitley?"

"Goddamn it all, you stupid hor..." Whitley pulled himself up to Chester's head, stroking his mane and staring into sightless eyes. "Dammit Chester. Why didn't you stop the bullets, or fly away, or toss all them Mounteds off the hill like a pile of gnats? You done got yourself shot, you... Damn you, Chester."

"Whitley? I'm sorry, Whitley. I'm sorry. I came back for you. I know you were angry, I know I don't understand things. Whitley?"

"We gotta get you out of here. Lift yourself up and let's get out of here, okay?" Whitley sat up on his knees struggling to lift Chester's head, "Come on now."

"Whitley? I'm scared, Whitley. I can feel everything."

"You been shot, Chester. Of course it's gonna hurt. Now get up!"

"Not pain, Whitley. Not me. I can feel everything. The trees whispering, the water flowing, the energy in the air. I feel it. I'm becoming it."

"What the hell kind of stupid... Just get up, damn you!"

"I'm sorry, Whitley. I'm sorry. Whitley. Whitley. Whitley."

Then nothing. Whitley felt nothing. The space in his head, where Chester's mind would echo, where he could reach out with invisible fingers and feel the ghost of that other mind. Gone.

The boots came heavy and fast from behind him, and by the time he returned to his conscious mind and felt the ground beneath him and the sound inside his own ears, they were all around him, guns drawn, Kendricks looming above him.

"Take him."

Then black.

****

Whitley came to staring up into the great expanse of the universe, stars gleaming above him in the night. He could smell the camp fire, and hear the laughter of Kendricks' men. He struggled to sit up, as his arms were bound behind him, and he coughed and sputtered as he came up, the sting of the blow that laid him out still burned at the base of his skull. He turned towards the source of the voices and shook cobwebs loose from his head, straining to bring his eyes together to focus and turn triple-vision into something he could make sense of.

"Kendricks! You no-good son of a whore!" he bellowed out into the night, "Kendricks!"

The laughter stopped. There was a slight murmur followed by the sounds of boots scuffling through the dirt as one of the men ran off to find their Captain.

Whitley's senses returned quickly, one after the other, clicking like switches on a railway line, connecting through his mind as the freight train of power that had been unlocked, barreled its way through, filling Whitley with a hum not unlike that he'd felt inside the strange cave. He felt Kendricks before he heard or saw him. He knew he had stopped at the fire and collected a plate, biding his time among the men, so as to assert his dominance over his prisoner. When he approached, it was with a tall trooper, who carried Whitley's brand new Winchester at arms.

"Well, well, well," Kendricks laughed, "did you have yourself a fine nap, Whitley?"

Whitley stared hard at the man, then sneered as he looked towards the one with the rifle.

"Ah, yes. A fine weapon. Many thanks for that, Whitley. I'm only sorry we failed to shoot you with it. Perhaps we'll employ it when we return to the fort in the morning. When you face the firing line as a foreign invader and wanted criminal."

Kendricks held the plate out towards Whitley, a grey slab of meat still sizzling at the center.

"Hungry? It's a little tough, but appreciated no less. My men have quite enjoyed it." A malicious grin worked its way across his face, the amusement at his own twisted joke desperate to be seen. "Took a while to find any part of that nag that wasn't too old and stringy to be edible, put we made sure to really take it to pieces. You don't mind do you?"

Whitley paled. Eyes widening as the fury spread through his body, he felt his hands freed, as if the ropes had disintegrated from his wrists. He could feel the crackling of energy in every part of his body, building to a boil, ready to explode in a blast of destructive steam at any moment. No. Not yet.

"You really should eat something Whitley. It will, most likely, be your last meal." Kendricks laughed again, wildly cackling as he tossed the plate at Whitley's feet.

Whitley worked a puddle in his mouth and spat at Kendricks feet, splashing the man's boots.

Kendricks immediately lunged forward with a fist. Whitley saw it in his mind's eye and easily moved his body out of the way, Kendricks pitching forward into the dirt, landing on his face, coming up bloody. The man with the rifle stepped forward and leveled it at Whitley, but Kendricks stood and waved him back before removing a kerchief to dab the blood from his face.

"You contemptible heathen!"

Whitley raised himself up slowly, fully in control of himself at last, finally seeing what Chester had meant by the stillness of his mind, knowing that he was so far beyond what Kendricks could comprehend. The rattle and clamor of Life, of his surroundings, of memory and sense and feeling, all of it came together into a barely-perceptible hum, which left his mind so quiet, so serene, after a lifetime of cacophony. Whitley understood now what was happening inside of him, as his brain opened up new pathways, new dark corners which had previously been locked away and silent. All of the Universe lay in front of him now, an understanding that should have left him mad and babbling. Instead, he had been given the means to not only comprehend, but control everything around him.

Whitley struck out with a thought, and the man at Kendricks side was flung through the air like a rag doll, tumbling a hundred yards through the air before landing with a thud in the darkness. No other sound followed, except the rifle slapping into the outstretched hand of its rightful owner.

Kendricks staggered backwards, hollering for his men. Whitley heard them—felt them—tossing down plates, stomping across the ground between them, weapons clattering, voices raised in compliance to their leader. Whitley felt the surge of their intent, and met it with a thought.

Stop.

It was as if they had been placed under glass like a rare flower or a mysterious insect, frozen in time and space, separated from the world at large. Whitley turned to appreciate the silence, feeling only contentment that his command had been answered and the men were no longer a consideration.

Kendricks stared, slack-jawed at the men, slapping their hands against an invisible barrier, screaming in confusion, wailing for guidance from their fearless commander.

"What? What the hell have you? What... what are you?" Kendricks stammered, fumbling backwards, away from Whitley, away from whatever Whitley had become.

Whitley, enjoying himself now, put one hand in front of him, reaching towards Kendricks and felt the air between them, the energy flowing from his hand to Kendricks body seven feet away. He picked Kendricks up off of his feet, suspending him in mid-air, forcing his arms outstretched as he had seen in so many pictures from so many biblical books—Jesus on the mount—watching Kendricks face widen and tremble in fear and astonishment as he hovered, helpless above the ground. Then he dropped him altogether. As easily as he had taken control of the space around Kendricks, the very space that was Kendricks, he relinquished control and let him crumble back to the earth.

Kendricks fell back hard onto his ass in the dirt. "No. No. What are you? Devil! American devil!"

"I'm a new man, Kendricks. A better man. A damn sight better than you, for certain."

Kendricks fumbled at his belt and came up with his pistol, aiming shakily and firing wild, screaming into the night as each shot seemed to bend away from its target and fall, impotent, in the dust.

Whitley laughed, stepping toward the terrified Kendricks with a smile.

"Go ahead, you filthy cur. Go ahead and kill me."

Whitley bent down and whispered in Kendricks ear. "That'd make as much sense as takin' a shotgun to a butterfly."

As he walked away into the shadows, Whitley heard Kendricks scrambling to reload his pistol.

"I'll get you, you foul demon, you unholy cur!" Kendricks shouted, "I'll hunt you till the day you die!"

The shots were like thunder in the emptiness of the prairie night. Whitley didn't need to hear them, nor did he need to see them to know where they were. Whitley felt everything now. Just like Chester had, right before he died. Right before Kendricks took him away.

Whitley felt the heaviness of the clouds, the rising electricity gathering above, even before the first raindrops began to fall. He even felt the bullets as they turned and sped back to their sender, tearing through Kendricks in a half dozen places, burning through his flesh like fire.

Whitley hung his head and waited for the rain, only wishing Chester was beside him.

LINER NOTES

Hot damn! Now wasn't that something.

Hey! Thanks for dropping by and hanging out with us on the wild frontier of the weird west. I know there seems to be a small underground surge of these kinds of books these days but, hell, we've been working on this thing for a couple of years now. Deadlines came and went, stories fell hither and yon, writers joined up and writers got gunned down in the street after being called out as yellow-bellied sonsawhores. We continued on, struggled through that remote pass, persevered through the long winter months of the in-between-times, and we came out on the other side of these mountains with only a few lost fingers and toes, and at least three pounds of frozen writer meat left to feed us. We've all agreed not to talk about it. What happens on Cannibal Mountain stays on Cannibal Mountain.

So first off, let me offer up my own thanks and a little round of applause for all of the writers involved, and give you a little rundown on their whys and wherefores and whathaveyous.

Jackson Lowry just happens to be the pen name of a prolific sumbitch who was born in Texas, raised in The West, and now wrangles words in the deserts of New Mexico. If we told you his real name, we'd have to scrape you up off of the floor before we killed you. Some say that his story in this tome may be based on unsubstantiated truth. Rumor has it that ol' Jacks has been seen gnawing on his share of pretty big damn steaks down there by Los Alamos. Whether that's one of those Godzilla-type nuclear accident kind-of situations, or prehistoric bronto burgers... who's to say? In any case, Lowry has no less than fifteen stories and novels out there under his brim, including the novel Great West Detective Agency and a new adult western in the Blaze! Series called Six-Gun Wedding. Jackson is also continuing his weird west ways in an upcoming trilogy with Western Trail Blazers, starting with the first book Undead. You can wander on down to www.jacksonlowry.com to find out more.

Bloodhound. Holy hairy hell in a handbasket. C. Courtney Joyner certainly knows how to bring the chills and thrills to the western setting. Ol' Court's widely known to be an expert on the Spaghetti Western, and has served as the movie editor for True West Magazine, as well as contributing to Round-Up, Famous Monsters of Filmland and Fangoria. He can even be heard offering audio commentary on rereleased classics like The Comancheros, The Grand Duel, and The Big Gundown, some of the greatest non-Eastwood films in the genre. Mr. Joyner is a well-known screenwriter, including some of the great cult classics of the 80's and 90's, including work on the Trancers and Puppet Master series, as well as William Shatner's Fright Night. He is also the author of a multitude of horror, western and crime stories, that have appeared in award winning anthologies like Law of the Gun, Hell Comes to Hollywood and Six Guns and Slay Bells. His hellacious genre-blasting novel Shotgun was nominated for a Peacemaker Award by the Western Fictioneers, and the follow-up, Shotgun 2: The Bleeding Ground is scheduled for October 2016. He's also working on a new adventure series for the good folks at Tor. What the hell he's doing hanging around here, we have no idea, but we sure are glad to have him. You can find Court at www.ccourtneyjoyner.com

El Cuchillo, the masked madman of the Pecos Andes. Or so he says. We aren't even sure that's a place... or a thing... "The Knife" cuts deep with his quick and dirty tale of bloodthirsty beasts on the range. His is also a pen name, obviously, but his real identity is just as vague and imperceptible. His history is as mysterious as his name. All I can tell you is that he delivered the groceries. The term "sloppy meat piñata" alone is destined to haunt your cerebellum for the foreseeable future. I liked this wily bastard so much, I let him write the introduction as well. And he assures me that he will return my grandmother and her dog, unharmed, once that introduction sees print. He doesn't have a website, or a place of residence. If you want to get in contact, just call up the Circle-K on the corner of 9th and Hennepin and ask for Nacho Laredo. He'll give you the number of a payphone somewhere in the vicinity of Chinatown, then you… well, let's just say that it goes on from there.

What can I say about Scott S. Phillips that I haven't said every damn time his name gets mentioned. I love this dude. He is the big brother I never knew I wanted, and he has been everywhere and done everything, man. He's been a screenwriter, a filmmaker, a movie critic, a librarian, a long-haired lothario, a Shakespearean hobo, a drive-thru connoisseur, a comic-book scribe, a purveyor of fine films, a mage, a sage, a pauper, a poet, a pawn and a king. You can find him hiding in the background of the original Red Dawn. He wrote the underground cult classics Drive (greatest American martial arts movie you've never seen) and Stink of Flesh (Best non-Romero zombie flick that you'd better go see right NOW, which Scott also directed). He wrote an official Friday the 13th tie-in novel. He once shared an apartment with Scream Queen Linnea Quigley. He wrote a comic book with Dirk Benedict, the Faceman himself! He once worked as a stand-in on a Motorhead video. For Lemmy. Fucking Lemmy. Scott S. Phillips is the coolest cat I know, and my A-#1 personal favorite wordsmith. I sure as hell was not going to put this book together without one of his tales of crime and self-destruction. The Gifts Of A Folding Girl delivers in spades, and bullets, and the best monkey-paw screw job in eons. Go find Scotty's fine tales of woe and whimsy, including Squirrel Eyes, Tales of Misery and Imagination, and Pete, Drinker of Blood. You should also check out his hilarious series of Boone Butters shorts on Amazon, and then get ready for Pete Has Risen From The Grave coming soon!

Grady Cole is another damned pen name. What is it with these dudes? Grady Cole is named for two young fellas who were somehow themselves unknowingly named for the Cormac McCarthy character. All four - the writer, the boys and the runaway Texas farm boy-turned-ranchero - prefer their whiskey straight, and their tales terrifying. You Are The Blood takes the old vampire standby, turns it on its head, grabs itself a real solid switch (probably a stripling of birch or poplar) and lays into that toothy sumbitch to show it who's boss. Grady Cole is currently under extreme pressure to do more work for Coffin Hop Press but, so far, he just wants to sit in the back of our office, drinking coffee out of the pot, reading Clive Barker and intermittently staring at a worn picture of naked Penelope Cruz. I can't really blame him.

Dinner at Carcosa, by Allan Williams, better known around Cowtown as Bassano del Grappa, auctioneer and raconteur at the former Gorilla House Art Gallery. We're not sure which of these names is his real one, but wherever he goes tall tales follow. Allan is new to short fiction, but long to the art of writing. A fine, well-seasoned journalist with his notepad pulled close to his snarling grizzled face, he's whispered to have written campaign speeches for cabinet ministers and once turned down work as a spy. I mean, what do you say to that? You say, "Give us the story and you can have the notepad back!" Why is he here - slumming for kicks, or angling for a story? Maybe it was all the whiskey we poured down his gullet in the name of Fiction. He loves his grandma's lavender tea. Check him out at www.CoffeeAndBlarney.com.

Rick Overwater is a wildly talented sonofagun. Rocker. Roller. Wordslinger. Another former journalisto turned slovenly fiction hack. Rick is the co-creator/writer of the comic book Futility, and singer/songwriter/guitar-basher in The County Reeves. If he ain't rockin', he's writing. He is currently working on some very cool stuff, including some steampunkish badassery involving Harry Houdini and the early days of deep sea diving. Cold Eggs and Whiskey is his first published short story, but you wouldn't know it by the taste. Dark, twisted and full of twang, this story was the impetus for the whole dang project. Rick was also conscripted as the resident copy editor and all-around asskicker for Coffin Hop Press. This book has his stink all over it, and damn if it don't smell like excellence. Rick is frequently found imbibing - and surviving - at www.overwater.ca

Craig Garrett is a beautiful Southern Gentleman who is most certainly too good for the likes of this book. His story Death Is Daily is a heartbreaking chunk of raw fiction gold. Fantasy and Western rarely meet so tenderly, or with such brutal sincerity. Craig is a former Professor of English and death row prison guard. I once watched him wrassle a bear. His beard is glorious. His fiction has been published in The Brooklyn Rail, Shotgun Honey, Fires on the Plain and Dark Moon Digest. He is the writer of the exceptional webcomic Robot Lincoln and Zombie Jackson. You can find him at @craiggarrett and ask him why he'd want to get mixed up with a bunch of yahoos like us.

Let's address that elephant in the corner. You see him. Right over there. Shifty eyes, trunk scarred with a lifetime of misery. Eating all the cheese puffs. He asks me "How did you get away with putting your own damn story in this book? What kind of self-serving, masturbatory, ego-driven bullshit is that?" Well, I'll tell you. I am the worst. Just the absolute worst. And also, we ran short on finished stories. This is the kind of thing that happens when you make anthologies. It's like a marathon. At the beginning, everybody's mom throws on her spanks, her spandex tights, her Juicy Couture and her brand-new neon pink Nike trainers with the filtered aeration system and the micro-pump actuators with the quadroponic blaupunkt. Whatever the fuck that might be. By the time you get to the finish line? Mrs. Delvecchio, with the tight abs and the pneumatic floatation devices; and Toby's scrawny mom who only eats Kale and farts like a wind farm. They're the only two who make it to the end. Everybody else goes home to rub lavender oil on their calves and call in to book a pedi. Such is Life. So. It. Goes. As such, I threw a little something into the mix to help us make weight. I think it turned out alright. The Horse Always Gets It First kinda feels like a Twilight Zone version of Sergio Corbucci. Scotty liked it. Blame him. If you do like it, go check out some of my other stuff, like the Arthur

Ellis Award nominated Hot Sinatra, once described as the Robert Rodriguez version of an Elmore Leonard book. I'll take it. Or check out the Manlove & Kickerdick Tricks, a bunch of short stories featuring two hired thugs who happen to also be a gender-specific couple, and underground sex performers, and really terrible at crime. Find it all at www.axelhow.com

Each and every one of us is a fan of the weird, a denizen of the outlands, and a lover of the hard-scrabble, do-or-die, six-guns and knife fights, horse-always-gets-it-first Wild West. Ain't we all? I know I've been a fan since as long as I can remember. Possibly even before my ol' Granddaddy told me tales of how I was distantly related to the Younger side of the James-Younger gang, how his own Grandpappy was run out of Missourah on a rail, how we came from cattle rustler and horse thieves before the good name of Howerton wandered on up north of the whiskey trail and settled down to ranch and farm in Southern Alberta, which is basically the Texas panhandle of the Great White North. I'm sure it was 98% bullshit, but it still gives me gumption. I grew up with cowboys, ranchers, farmers and oilmen. My cousins were chuck wagon racers and rodeo riders. My Granddad wore boots every day of his life, and if he wasn't wearing his Stetson, he was wearing that green John Deere trucker cap. And when he wasn't wearing the Stetson, I was drowning myself in its ten gallon cavern. When I was ten, I stayed up all night watching Sergio Leone flicks, spent all my summer afternoons slinging hot plastic from the hip and watching Wanted: Dead or Alive reruns on the UHF channels. I may have been a kid through the 70's and 80's, and been obsessed with sci-fi TV shows, horror movies, Harryhausen monster flicks, Ray Bradbury books, old Elmore Leonard westerns, the glory of Forrest J. Ackerman's Famous Monsters of Filmland magazine, and the mind-altering curves on Pam Grier, but underneath it all I was still that little rugrat with his Granddad's straw cattleman floating around his cheeks. Eventually all of those interests flow together, meld and merge, and become a mighty cheese monster, a veritable Horta spiced liberally with hickory and left on the front porch of the nearest farmhouse. Your twisted, abnormal writer-brain starts thinking "vampire showdown at high noon", or "psycho killer on the plains", or "James Bond and Indiana Jones meet ID4".

Wait. What? Well, at least two of those tales turned out pretty goddamn slick. In any case, I'm positive that if you asked any of these other guys, they'd tell you a similar story. Some of those stories I'm already privy to. Rick was an Alberta farm boy, still is, now he writes a comic about a farmer being molested by a nympho space slug. Jackson is Lone Star born and bred and dreaming up sexy school marms and undead gunslingers. Craig moved onto his own grandparents' farm and lives there to this day, spinning yarns and raising barns. Scotty occasionally wears chaps to breakfast. Ol' Court, hell, he's teaching the master class on Old West in modern pop culture. And Cuchillo? That mean old bastard eats rattlesnake with his beans and then scratches his stories out in the dust with their backbones. Each and every one of us has some touchstone connection to the myths and melodies of the Wild West and now we've birthed our mutant hybrid half-calf alien symbiote upon you all.

I, for one, welcome our new alien trail bosses.

Adios, muchachos and muchachas.
Sleep tight, don't let the Chupacabras bite

-Axel Howerton

More from

Coffin Hop Press

Coffin Hop Press

NEGATIVE

Blood Can Be As Black As Oil...

Tales of sin and corruption
from the darkest depths
of the dangerous
Canadian prairies

An Alberta Noir Anthology

Coffin Hop Press

AUGUST 2015

Made in the USA
Charleston, SC
01 April 2015